Long Grey Beard and Glittering Eye

Long Grey Beard and Glittering Eye

The Fiction Desk Anthology Series
Volume Nine

Edited by Rob Redman

The Fiction Desk

First published in 2015 by The Fiction Desk Ltd.

ISBN 978-0-9927547-5-4

The Fiction Desk
PO Box 116
Rye
TN31 9DY

Please note that we do not accept postal submissions.
See our website for submissions information.

www.thefictiondesk.com

The Fiction Desk Ltd
Registered in the UK, no 07410083
Registered office: 3rd Floor, 207 Regent Street, London, W1B 3HH

Printed and bound in the UK by TJ International, Cornwall.

Contents

Contents

Introduction

Rob Redman

Long grey beard and glittering eye: the combination of life experience and charisma that together make for the best stories.

The first is the raw material of fiction, whether it consists of experiences written down almost as they happened, or the accumulation of moments lived through, people met, and relationships of all kinds experienced and observed. The importance of personal experience in writing fiction can be taken rather too literally, but also dismissed too completely: from closely autobiographical fiction to a more general insight into the underlying mechanisms of human interaction, experience is gained and applied in as many ways in writing as it is in life. (This is why the old advice to authors to 'write what you know' is true, but also vague almost to the point of uselessness.)

So much for the long grey beard. The glittering eye of the original poem has been interpreted as charisma and/or madness (there being sometimes a rather fine line between the two). Another theory suggests that the glitter in the mariner's eye results from a hardening of the corneas after a lifetime spent staring into the wind from the deck of his ship, but for our purposes we'd better take it to stand for the ability to first capture and then hold the audience's attention.

Combine experience and charisma and you have, hopefully, a story that will capture the imagination from the first word to the last.

In the current volume we have no fewer than nine ancient mariners to keep you from your wedding feast. You may have read work by Die Booth, S R Mastrantone, Matthew Licht, and Richard Smyth in some of our previous anthologies. The others are all new to us, including Mark Newman and Tim Dunbar, who took first and second place in The Newcomer Prize, the annual competition that we started last year to encourage short story writing and help us to discover new talent.

Die Booth is one of The Fiction Desk's most prolific contributors, providing stories to both our supernatural collections and our general fiction anthologies. If you've not yet read Die's work, 'Whole Wide World' is a great place to start.

Whole Wide World

Die Booth

'Hold it by the edges, see.'

'Why?' Gareth held the record carefully by the edges anyway, turning it awkwardly in his hands.

'Because if you hold it flat you get all muck in the grooves and you might scratch it,' said Dad. Gareth nodded seriously and handed the LP back to Dad with exaggerated care, watching him place it on the turntable.

Playing a record was a bit of an event. Every weekend, Gareth nagged Dad to let him listen, and Dad performed the ceremony, removing the piles of books off the top of the cabinet, pushing back the hinged wooden lid, lifting the smoky plastic cover off the top of the turntable, and carefully fitting the vinyl before finally flipping a million switches and easing the stylus arm onto the very edge of the record to hiss and pop into music.

This was his favourite song, the one he always asked Dad to put on: 'Whole Wide World' by Wreckless Eric. Gareth wasn't sure about girls, but Tahiti had the same exotic ring to it as Swansea; he'd probably go there when he grew up, just to check whether what the song said was true. He might even live there.

Outside, relentless sunshine parched the hillside to fawn. The fields were dusty at the edges, but the little patch of lawn in front of their house had a sprinkler going at all times, maintaining the snooker-table greenness as a matter of family pride. Gareth tilted the big square record sleeve and considered the man on the front gravely. *Eric*, he thought, *that must be Eric.* He looked sort of like the coolest man in the world, and sort of like Dad. Dad was called John, but everyone called him Lewis, even though there were a lot of Lewises in the village. One day when Gareth was grown up, he'd be called Lewis and he'd live in Tahiti and have his own house and wife and lawn sprinkler.

Dad sat down on the sofa, listening to the music, but Gareth stayed standing so he could watch the disc wobble round in gentle, undulating waves. He leaned against Dad's knees and asked, 'Why do you have records?'

'Because they sound better than tapes.'

Gareth considered this. He knew all about cassette tapes. He had his own portable cassette recorder with a carry handle and a microphone and he made C90 mix tapes, recording with determined concentration from the radio during every Sunday teatime pop chart countdown. He'd become an expert with the pause button, skilled and perfectionist; it aggravated him beyond reason to catch any of the DJ's between-track patter on tape.

Sometimes he recorded other things too. He had a whole tape dedicated to random noises he liked, which he recorded with his microphone: Ben and Toy barking, the sound of the cereal-box spokey dokeys on his spinning bike wheels, snippets of television and tractor rumbles and Dad's loud, rude laugh. And sometimes he set his cassette recorder up facing the speakers of Mum and Dad's sound system that was stacked up on shelves beneath the record player, and re-recorded off played-back tapes of songs and sounds, mixing the two up in a continuous stream of chart hits and punk and sound bites and noises that got fainter and more furry with every re-recording. He'd invented that. Nobody in the world had ever, ever thought to record a mix tape off a mixture of mix tapes before. But, 'They do sound better than tapes,' he said to Dad. 'Why do you listen to tapes, then?'

Dad held up a seven-inch single, 'Identity' by X-Ray Spex. 'Imagine trying to fit that in your Walkman.'

It was true. Records were big and heavy to carry around, but Gareth didn't really care about things like that. 'I like them better,' he said, decidedly. Dad smiled.

'You're a funniosity, Gaz.'

'*You're* a funniosity.' Gareth said, grinning as he flipped for the tenth time that day through the stack of vinyl on the living room floor.

So far, he's never made it any further than Ibiza.

Now, Lewis holds his CDs by the edges, but he's still got his father's twelve-inch of 'Whole Wide World' tucked like a pressed flower between the Techno and Breakcore and Progressive Breakcore in his record crates. When he pictures him now, he's just called John again and his face, in Lewis's memory, is superimposed by Wreckless Eric's. Lewis isn't sure where he is now. Part of him suspects (*hopes*, Lewis thinks, but he'd never say that out loud) that John's out there somewhere in Tahiti, promising every pretty girl he meets that one day he'll introduce them to his long-lost son.

It's funny how things turn out.

How quickly things can change, can turn on a pin. A safety pin, 1977 style; stuck through a card, tacked to the wall behind a DJ booth then ripped in two and binned, but not completely forgotten.

'I'm off out,' says Lewis from the doorway. 'Won't be late, it's just a gig.'

Cam twists around on the couch, expels a yap of derisive laughter.

'Who's playing, Jeffree Starr?'

Lewis holds up one neon-gloved hand and flips him the finger.

'Nah, just a local thing. Bad Bones.'

'What's that then, dubstep?'

'Punk.'

Cam raises his eyebrows, but doesn't pass comment.

'Who you going with?'

'Who are you, my mum?'

'I meant,' Cam sighs. 'It doesn't matter.'

'I'm meetin' a mate there. Be gettin' the last train back but it'll probably be, like, one or something. It's a bit out of town.'

'Out of town?'

'Past Hampstead,' Lewis says, which is technically the truth: Uxbridge is quite a way past Hampstead on the Metropolitan Line. He's fitting his key in the door as Cam calls,

'Just, you know. If you can't be good be careful.'

'Back 'bout midnight,' Lewis shouts, slamming the door.

It's fine on the way to Liverpool Street and it's fine on the knee-jogging journey across the city, but by the time Lewis is walking down a suburban high street towards his destination and receiving a fair few curious looks, he starts to wonder if he hasn't dressed up in order to pick a fight. When he gets to the place, he stands outside long enough to smoke three cigarettes, each lit off the last one's filter.

It's a pub, an old-man pub, called the General Elliott. It's got benches out the front and cars parked and the whole thing is covered in white cladding like a Toby Carvery full of Sunday afternoon families; but the strains of music coming from inside are reassuringly guitar-driven.

He's been checking the gig listings in Uxbridge for a few weeks now.

Bad Bones: small circuit punk band from 1982. Lewis isn't sure what he's going to achieve coming here on his own to listen to music he's not even into any more, but suspects that it'll likely involve a punch-up, which might go some way to clearing his head and so, he reasons, will be achievement enough.

Sure enough, the moment he steps into the cramped main bar, all fox-hunting prints on the walls and polished brass and a little stage area cordoned off at the end by electrical tape markings on the sticky carpet, heads turn his way. He avoids eye contact and weaves to the bar. He'd like a beer but the bloody-minded kamikaze in him orders a watermelon Bacardi Breezer even though he hates them when they're not frozen first: anything to not have to throw the first punch.

And then he looks up across the sea of heads — middle-aged, middle-income, leather-jacketed blokes with thickening waists and thinning hair — and like some kind of stupid magic, he sees him.

'What the fuck's that?' says Nigel. He gestures over towards the bar with the hand holding his bottle of Newcastle Brown and smiles, not maliciously. John follows his direction and thinks, for a split second as his eyes register the colour and shape, *what a bloody state*. 'Kids, eh?' says Nigel, and chuckles. 'I hope his gob ain't as loud as his clobber or he might be gettin' carried out.' He says, 'John?' John doesn't reply. 'Mate? You look like you seen a ghost.'

'That's my son,' says John.

It's the most awkward and the easiest thing in the world.

'Long time no see,' John says, after he's side-walked elbows-first across to where Lewis is standing.

'Alright?' says Lewis, then the words seem to thicken and stick, so they just stand for a while, watching the band thrash out a couple of middle-of-the-road songs until John leans up and shouts,

'You want to go outside?'

It's freezing out the front. Lewis pulls his coat with the fur collar around him and the seat of the picnic bench is so cold that it feels like wet seeping into the seat of his jeans. He passes John a fag and John says,

'You still smoke,' but it's not a question and he doesn't sound surprised. He's never seen Lewis smoke, but then he's not seen Lewis in person since he was thirteen and any news of his habits since has been passed on via stilted telephone conversations with his ex-wife, which had themselves stopped just before Lewis turned seventeen. That must be... how many years ago? A lot of years. 'What you doin' here then?' John asks and Lewis says,

'Looking for you.' He blows a smoke ring and narrows his kohl-lined eyes, 'Just checked the listings round here for a few weeks and waited for a punk gig. I didn't think you'd really be here. I just, like...'

Hoped? John doesn't say it though, he just nods, sucking his teeth.

'It's good to see you, Gaz.'

'Nobody calls me that now.'

'And what do they call you, now?'

'Lewis.'

John looks down at his lap. 'Well that's a funny thing see, because now people just call me John.'

'Right.'

'I'll have to get used to callin' you Lewis then, won't I.'

'You don't have to. I don't care.'

'Then I expect you'll be callin' me John now.'

'Fuckin' hell...' he slaps the flat of his hand down on the bench; they both jump.

'What?'

'I can't... call you *John*. Jesus. Dad.'

It's horrible. Lewis wants to crawl out of his skin. He hides behind a faked cough that tries to dislodge the burn that's come up in his throat because the urge to lamp the prick and the urge to hug him are fighting so hard in his chest. John looks the same, but totally different. Totally different, but Lewis would recognise him anywhere all the same. The weirdest thing is how much shorter he seems, although obviously it's just Lewis has grown taller, a fair few inches taller now than his father. He remembers his dad with a black flat top and rockabilly chops but now John's hair is grey and falling just over his ears and he's wearing steel framed glasses. Lewis says, 'You got well fat.'

'You wait, it'll get you as well.'

'Not if I can help it. Least you still got all your hair.'

'Looks like you're missing some of yours.'

Lewis ducks as his father aims fingers at the shaved side of his head. He tries really, really hard not to smile. It shouldn't be this easy. He shouldn't let him off this easy. John says, 'So, did you get my card then?'

'Which one? The one you sent to the club, or the one for my seventeenth?'

'Ah, Gaz...'

'Yeah, I got it. I binned it.'

John nods. 'So why did you come to find me then?'

'Why did you send me a Christmas card? How'd you know where I work? Why now?'

John pinches the bridge of his nose, pushing his glasses up with thumb and forefinger. 'It wasn't... well, I didn't know where you were for a start.'

'Oh, bullshit! You could of found me! Aunty Joan's still livin' the same place, Nain's got... well...'

'Have you seen her?'

'Have *you* seen her?'

'No. How is she?'

'Fucking hell. You're a proper piece of shit, ain't you?'

'Yes.'

'Thirteen years, Dad.'

'I'm so sorry, Gaz. I was a fool. I started travelling and the time just passed me by.'

'I don't...' Lewis really doesn't. He doesn't know what to say. Any anger he had boiling deep down when he headed out tonight has simmered off or been replaced by some indefinable something-else. 'I don't care. I just don't give a shit, stay or go. I'm past caring.'

'Well, I deserve that.'

'You deserve a smack in the face.'

'I do.'

'Oh for fuck sake, stop bein' so...' the words won't come out, so Lewis kicks the leg of the table instead and it doesn't make him feel the slightest bit better. 'Just change the subject.'

'How's work?'

'Fine. I got my own club.'

'You what now? Are you shittin' me? I saw your name and your photo in that events listing doo-dah, but I thought you just worked there.'

No matter what the man says, Lewis wants to talk about something else.

'What you been up to then? For the past thirteen years?'

'This an' that. Did some labouring. Drove trucks. Played in a band, the bass — I don't suppose much your type of music now, mind.'

'What do you know about it?'

'Nothin' much,' John says quickly, 'only what was in that magazine, where I got your work address.'

'You married?'

'Oh no. No, I never remarried.'

'You been on your own for thirteen years?'

He shakes his head, his thumb rubbing circles on the knee of his jeans. 'Well, no. There's been a few... you know.' Lewis knows. He accidentally catches John's eye and they're so similar in some ways that it's a little frightening. 'How's your mum?'

'Good. Happy. You don't try and get in touch.'

'Okay... okay, I wouldn't dare. She's remarried then?'

Lewis hates what he's reading into John's tone.

'No. But she will be, yeah. She's with someone. Someone proper good lookin' an' young.'

'Oh yes?'

'He's got four kids.'

'Well, Christ. She'll be loving that. How old?'

'Twenty-three.'

'No, him, not the kids.'

'I'm *talking* about him.'

'Christ. Jesus.'

The silence stretches out between them, itchy with chain-smoke. John taps his ash into the central hole of the table where the big Stella Artois garden umbrella pokes through, because there's no ashtrays, and he says,

'So. You're a gay now, is it?' and Lewis nearly chokes on his drink.

'I'm with...' *I'm with a bloke, yeah.* It sounds sort of like a denial when he puts it like that, so Lewis says, 'Yeah. I'm gay,' and spies out from under his eyelashes to scrutinise John's face for disapproval.

John raises his eyebrows, but he doesn't look really disapproving. More resigned. He says, 'So how does that work, then?'

'Fuckin' hell, you want a diagram?'

'Oh, funny, lad. No, I mean — you was always one for the ladies, even in school wasn't you? I'm just shocked is all, I'm not judgin'.'

'Right.'

'Cut me some slack, now. I lived through punk, I've seen things would make your hair curl. An' besides,' John pushes the spent filter of his cigarette down through the hole in the table with one stubby finger, running the nail around the splintered edges. 'The way I see it, I got no room to be tellin' you how to live your life seein' as I've not been here for half of it.'

'Damn right.'

'So,' John nods his head towards the pub door, where a group of three is huddled, smoking rollies, and Lewis follows his glance, 'how about him then, in the Ruts jacket, is he good lookin'?'

Lewis's laugh catches him by surprise, loud, and he ducks his head as one of the men by the door looks over at him. John says, 'No? His mate then who just gave you the eyeball, is he tidy? Nice arse, eh?'

'Shittin' hell — Dad — no!' It's out now though, the smile. 'Shut up, you mental, you'll get us filled in! I'm with someone, I don't fancy random crusty blokes.'

'Skinhead more your type, then?' says John, but he's grinning. 'I'm out. They got a fag machine in there, you notice? Am I still allowed to say "fag"?'

'Shut it.'

'Come on, I'm freezin' to death an' dyin' of thirst here. I'll buy you one of your pink lady drinks.'

'Yeah, a bottle of Newky'll do, cheers.'

His head is spinning so much on the train home that Lewis isn't sure it's just the beer and the guitar decibels. If anything, he feels weirdly sober as he fits his key in the door and tries to keep the noise down, rattling the uncooperative lock to let himself in.

'Lewis?'

Lewis stops, paused on the second step up the stairs. Cam's still up, although the living room's dark: peering around the door he sees the bluish glow of a laptop screen and Cam sprawled across the couch, rubbing his eyes with the back of his hand. The room smells like stale beer and carpet. Lewis walks in and tugs the throw that serves as a curtain across the front window, blocking the lamp-lit street out.

'Cam,' he says, 'I got summat to tell you.'

Cam's voice is soft with more than sleep. 'That doesn't sound good.'

'About tonight...'

'Oh.' His hands are over his eyes now. Lewis kneels down and pulls them away, but Cam places them back, like not seeing will make it not real. He says, 'You were meeting a guy.'

'No.' Lewis tips his chin up and this time the hands stay down. 'Well... yeah, but not like that. Listen. I got to play you something.'

The sound of flipping through vinyl is a little like remembered playing cards in bike wheels; there's somehow something of childhood in it, at any rate. Cam shuffles round to watch him. When he finds it, pulls out the tatty sleeve and shows him, Cam says, 'He's back,' and the words hold no surprise. Only music.

NOTICE: *The following story contains observations regarding the impact of technological change and social media on society and interpersonal relationships.*

To acknowledge this notice and read the story, please blink once...

Thank you.

I Don't Blink

Jacki Donnellan

I can almost feel it, even before I see it. All their busy, darting eyes, flickering past me before they stop and track back to focus on me.

They blink.

Stare.

Follow me, if I move.

Blink.

Mutter something, smile, blink again.

As for me, I don't blink. And it makes me stand out.

Of course, my eyelids are shutting involuntarily every few seconds, so that my eyes don't dry out. Actual blinking. Not the deliberate, rapid-fire sort that everyone else is doing. *Clinking.*

Blink-to-click. Blink to start video, capture speech, and blink to post. Blink-to-click. *Clink.*

I wonder what's being said about me, now, on *Flutter* or *Eye-Contact* or whichever social media page I've just been uploaded to. 'Guy wiv NO W'Eye-fi! Looks sooo bored, lol!' perhaps, beneath a gif of my unblinking eyes.

I shuffle awkwardly from foot to foot and try my best to keep looking down. The floor and the walls here are all plain white and actually, I am rather bored. I try and think about something else and inevitably, memories of Sarah begin to slide effortlessly across my mind.

'Are you really sure you could never do it, Rob?' she is saying, her voice like chocolate. 'Don't you think it would be exciting?' And she takes my arm and nuzzles my ear as we stroll down the street, giggling as we pass a Distant Gaze camera on the corner.

My answer was always the same. 'No.'

I would tell her that I had no absolutely no interest in W'Eye-fi, and that having a pair of W'Eye Glasses was quite enough for me, thank you very much. And Sarah had liked that about me, at first. I think she found me special; saw me as a man who didn't follow the crowd.

Or possibly that was how *I* saw me. Maybe she just found me quaint.

Gosh, this queue is moving slowly. In fact I'm surprised there's a queue at all; I imagined the process would be a much quicker affair. I try and peer around at the front of the queue and see a girl with piercing emerald eyes coming towards me. She heads past me to the exit and looks back into the room as she leaves. Her eyes, I notice, have become a bright shade of purple.

I tut, and roll my eyes. It's the latest thing; W'Eye Colour, I believe it's called. I even saw a girl with eyes that quite literally sparkled the other day. And of course they were nothing compared to a pair of naturally lovely eyes, such as Sarah's. Sarah's eyes even shone like sapphires behind her W'Eye Glasses.

So I didn't really notice, at first, when she began to wear her W'Eye Glasses more and more. And then she synced her pair to mine and we enabled Double Vision, and sharing what we saw did seem to bring us closer.

But after a while I noticed that she was beginning to clink open some of those peripheral promos. *Open your eyes to W'Eye-fi! Installed in the blink of an eye!* The ones I'd advised her to ignore.

'I thought we discussed this, Sarah,' I said one day. 'You agreed you would never go down that ridiculous route of implants and lens boards.'

She didn't reply. Instead, my W'Eye Glasses went fuzzy for a moment, and then I realised that not only was she not replying to my message, she had disabled Double Vision.

The queue moves forward a little. I can see a white door, now, to which the queue is headed. I'm amazed, quite frankly, by the lack of staff here. Not even a receptionist to greet people!

'*Look*,' Sarah would hiss, in those days towards the end, when her voice had set permanently hard. 'Just put on your W'Eye Glasses and *look*, for pity's sake! Why do you insist on wandering around in ignorance, when we arrive somewhere new? There'll be a menu, or a map — there'll be some visual overlay that will tell you what to do, so you don't have to stand there looking gormless, like you're doing.'

And although I didn't enjoy it when she spoke to me like that, I adored the way her cheeks would blaze a gorgeous shade of pink when she was angry. And I tried to keep things between us alive; I wore my W'Eye Glasses a bit more, hoping that might make her happy, and tried not to irritate her by tutting whenever I got those annoying peri-promos in my W'Eye.

But we were talking less and less. Eventually I felt barely closer to her than the rest of the world, only able to share with her what she was willing to share publicly on her Eye-Contact page. If I suggested that we should sync our W'Eye Glasses again she would murmur something about doing it later. But she never did.

The queue is shorter now. Progress, at last! Though I'm not completely sure, of course, if I'm in the right place, or whether I even need to go through that white door. I consider asking the people in front of me in the queue, but they are a bunch of teenage lads who have clearly synced their W'Eye-fi to Group Vision, as they're all staring into space and guffawing in unison.

I resort to taking my W'Eye Glasses out of my pocket, and putting them on.

It takes a few seconds for my eyes to adjust — the Glasses probably aren't aligned with my eyesight any more — and then I look around at the transformed room in front of me. The walls are seething with adverts, and peri-promos twinkle for attention down the left side of the room. My App Portal is revolving up in the corner — not worth clinking on that now that most W'Eye Glass apps are defunct — and there, in front of me, is a menu.

I look at the menu and try to navigate, but suddenly there is a blonde, buxom woman gyrating her hips in front of me, wearing nothing but a very small thong.

I watch her for a few seconds before I come to my senses, and tap the shoulder of the young man in front of me.

'Excuse me,' I say. 'Would you mind turning down the field of your Group Vision? It's interfering with my own field.'

For a moment the young man doesn't register that he's being spoken to, but then he notices me. His face widens into an amused grin when he sees that I'm wearing W'Eye Glasses.

'You need to isolate yo' own field, innit, Grandad?' he says, and turns back to his friends.

'I'm thirty-seven, actually,' I mutter. I have no idea how to isolate my own field. I try to clink on the menu without looking at the undulating woman in front of it or the pole around which she's now entangled, but I can't see the menu clearly enough.

And then everything freezes, and no matter how much I clink, the room remains a motionless mass of colour with a topless woman spread-eagled along a pole in the centre of it.

I sigh, and take off my W'Eye Glasses. They've been glitching like that for a while now.

'Of course I don't need to upgrade them,' I'd said to Sarah, 'I haven't had them long. And there's certainly no need to just throw the glasses away and switch blindly to W'Eye-fi, if you'll pardon the pu–'

'Fine!' Sarah yelled, throwing up her hands in mock surrender. 'Just sit there forever with your W'Eye Glasses on like a stupid, specky dinosaur, while the rest of the world moves on and passes you by!'

'I'm certainly not stupid,' I said. 'I'm thinking for myself. Do you even know how it works, this W'Eye-fi? Or what the long-term effects are of attaching things to your eyes, or even how they're attached? And how those "neural connectors" (I drew the inverted commas in the air with my forefingers) even work?'

Sarah gave a derisive laugh. 'I'm an accounts manager,' she scoffed, 'of course I don't know how they work! If I only used things if I knew how they worked I'd never even use the microwave.'

Then she lapsed into one of her long, stubborn silences, during which I yearned both to roar at her in frustration, and cover her in tender kisses.

I'm nearly at the front of the queue now. The white door opens, and the lads in front of me all pile in. I try and peek in, just to check that I'm in the right place, but the door slams shut in my face.

Rather like my own front door, on that Thursday about six months ago.

After watching Sarah pack, I'd followed her forlornly along the hallway, and when she'd opened the front door and turned back to face me I had placed my question carefully in front of her, like a neatly folded shirt: 'Can we still be friends?'

She looked at me and said, 'Sorry. I've moved on. You should too.'

And with a slam of the door, she was gone.

And how I wished that I'd been wearing my W'Eye Glasses, so as to have taken one last photo before she went! And I confess that I wore my W'Eye Glasses constantly in the days that followed, the way I tried never to do, just in case Sarah contacted me, if only to tell me where she'd gone.

Eventually I tried reaching her at work, and even attempted to access her Eye-Contact page, hoping we could at least be friends electronically. But she had blocked me from her life, utterly and completely.

The white door has now opened again. I step forward and walk through to find a disarmingly young, rather plump girl sitting at a white table, in another all-white room.

The girl's clinking eyes cease for a moment as she looks at me, obviously thrown by someone who has made no connection with her electronically.

'Um, this room is for Lens Upgrades,' she says.

'Lens... upgrades?' I repeat, rather infuriated at how unintelligent I must sound.

'Yes. I'm an Upgrade Technician,' she says, pointing at something invisible in front of her chest, until her eyes look up to meet mine. 'Oh,' she says, 'your W'Eye-fi's down.' She begins speaking loudly and slowly, as if I might be deaf. 'Sorry, but you're in the WRONG DEPARTMENT. *Repairs* is FURTHER ALONG; you should have come in through the OTHER ENTRANCE. This is UP-GRADES.'

Then she turns and stares at the wall.

'Well actually,' I explain, 'I don't have W'Eye-fi at all.'

Her head whips round and she looks at me as if I have just displayed a deeply personal medical ailment.

'Um,' she says, with an embarrassed smile, 'then you need to be next door.' She begins staring at the wall again, and I realise there are doors in it. She blinks, and one of them opens. 'You can go the back way, through there.'

I nod my thanks and walk through the door, into another room.

This room is filled with people; mostly families. 'Welcome to the W'Eye-fi clinic' is printed in cheerful colours across the wall, and a huge blue glass W'Eye-fi symbol (the @ sign with four eyelashes above it) is suspended from the ceiling. W'Eye Glassed tweenagers are trying to look bored despite their obvious excitement at being here, while younger siblings chatter and weave around their parents like bespectacled maypole ribbons.

'How do you feel about children?' Sarah once asked me, way back in the days when we had just begun dating. I can remember that her hair was like bright, copper swirls around her face, but I can't remember, now, what I said in reply.

Because I find myself suddenly rather distracted by the memory of what happened in the toyshop, last week; the reason that I am here.

It was last week that I'd finally emerged from six months of disorientated fug after my break-up with Sarah. And I'd decided that I was going to re-assemble my life into the comfortably beige place that it had been before Sarah had come along and peppered it with glitter. I was going to move on, my way. And this would include having my W'Eye Glasses repaired, so they could continue to meet all my needs perfectly adequately.

I was surprised, I admit, once I realised that only toyshops and geriatric-aid suppliers really deal in W'Eye Glasses any more. But I was undeterred. I had a shave, got a haircut, and went to a toyshop, where I began confidently seeking out the customer service desk.

I marched with determination past shelves crammed with army-green W'Eye-to-W'Eye Combat Glasses, and nerdy black Wiki Tell-Me-W'Eye Glasses.

But when I got to an aisle full of pink and blue Teeny Tiny W'Eyeny Glasses, I stood stock still in slack-jawed surprise.

Because right in front of me, gliding slowly between the shelves, was Sarah.

She had her back to me, looking down with quiet concentration at the shelves as she moved slowly past them, her eyes occasionally blinking.

I didn't blink. I barely breathed. I just stood there, silently quenching my thirst with the sight of her. She looked just as beautiful as I remembered, and yet there was something slightly different about her; something I couldn't quite place.

I waited until I felt ready, and then I said:

'Hello, Sarah.'

She flinched. She turned to face me as she did so, and that was when I saw; when I realised how she had changed.

There was an exquisite and enormous roundness to her tummy, which had always been exquisite, but never enormous and certainly not round.

'O my gosh,' I blurted, as Sarah gasped, and began to run.

'Wait! Sarah! Is it...? I mean...'

I began chasing her through the toyshop. I remember thinking that she was surprisingly quick for someone who was around seven months pregnant, if I had calculated, assumed, and hoped correctly.

'Just leave me alone!' she yelled over her shoulder, still running. I followed her as she turned and sped down the vintage aisle.

'Sarah, wait!' I pleaded. I began to run faster. I had almost caught up with her when suddenly she stopped, reached behind her and pulled desperately at the bottom row of an enormous display-mountain of space hoppers. The mountain immediately crumbled into a huge space-hopper avalanche, and I found myself helplessly tripping and tumbling in amongst it.

'Sarah!' I cried, rather pathetically, as a multitude of space hoppers bounced and bobbed all around me like an army of jolly, inflated bellies, knocking me off balance each time I tried to stand.

I managed to look up just in time to see Sarah, all blooming and full of the future, heading swiftly out of the shop.

And as I flailed about in a sea of joggling, goofy space hopper faces, I could have almost sworn that they were laughing, and that every last pair of their big, googly space hopper eyes was blinking.

It's my turn, now.

I am lying back, in a dentist-style chair. The Installation Technician leans over me and squeezes a clear liquid into each eye.

'So,' he says, 'the W'Eye Spy app that you've requested will be ready in your App Portal just as soon as you're live. Just clink on the Portal, then clink the app to open.'

'Okay,' I say. The liquid in my eyes is trickling down my cheeks. 'And to find someone's location...?'

'Just clink on the Gaze-Tracker menu, and you'll find them in the blink of an eye.'

He gives me a small smile and what looks like a wink, but perhaps he's just checking his Eyemails.

'Right, here we go,' he says, leaning towards my eye with what looks like a large barbed screwdriver.

I wonder what it is?

A girl, as dazzling and enchanting as her mother?

'That's right,' says the technician, 'eyes nice and wide, ready, and...'

I keep my eyes open. I don't blink.

S R Mastrantone's third Fiction Desk story continues his exploration of the tensions that lie between thinking and doing in everyday life. In our next anthology, he'll be taking a turn towards the supernatural.

Just the Stars to Look Up To

S R Mastrantone

When I ran out of real role models, I started to make them up.

There was this skinny white bloke, in his forties maybe, who sat on the opposite train platform to me in the morning. He wore a long beige coat, and glasses that were too small for his face. I'd wait for the train to Birmingham and watch him wait for the train to London, and I'd imagine what he got up to there. Maybe he was some high-powered lawyer for the rich and famous, and his little black briefcase contained folders filled with salacious secrets. Or maybe he worked in the Houses of Parliament, fighting the system from within. Or what if he worked for the Secret Service, and that briefcase hid a vial of poison destined for the drink of some unsuspecting member of al Qaeda?

Whatever he really did, he was my new hero. Because like me he lived around Marlstone — maybe he still had friends or family here, or whatever — but also like me he knew Marlstone wasn't the real world. That's why he spent three hours a day commuting. He wanted to be with all the other proper people. London people.

The big city is like a magnet for that sort. People who see things through to the end and stick to their plans, who don't just give up at the first hurdle. High achievers. Dreamers.

One day I would be like him. I'd get up, cross the bridge to the other platform, and get on the train to London. I knew people there: friends of friends, my dad's second cousin Mally. Maybe they were just being nice when they said they'd help me out. But in my imagination they would all throw open their doors, grin at me and say, 'Parvez, what took you so long?'

Around Marlstone, everyone was a disappointment. I'd been tiptoeing around the fragments of other people's broken commitments for a while.

My parents split up four years ago. At the time it never felt that important. They'd been arguing so much that when my dad broke the news on the way to school I said, 'Thank God,' and he laughed. I even started to imagine all the cool places one of them might choose to live in: New York, Paris, London.

Both of them stayed in Marlstone.

I lived with Dad first. It was easier because he lived on the bus route. How could Mom be upset about that? But if I'm honest, I did prefer the idea of living with Dad. He never gave me hassle and he liked good music. He'd even restarted his old punk band, shaved off what was left of his hair and got his ear pierced. I went to watch them rehearse — they were decent.

I used to think he was a great bloke. Once, when I was really young, some kid took the piss out me for having big ears. When I told my Dad he just said that people who had time to think about looks didn't have anything meaningful to fill their heads with, and that I should feel sorry for them for being so dull. It was such good advice, because nothing annoys a bully more than pity. He'd had experience himself with bullies. Growing up Pakistani in the Midlands during the seventies, he went through things much worse than I've ever been through. That's not to say that Marlstone doesn't still have its racists. They just hide better.

I never saw him much, once it was just him and me. He was out with all these different women and Mom kept saying he was having a mid-life crisis, and that he'd regret it all when he sobered up. We lived in a top-floor maisonette around the back of the train station, not far from an Indian restaurant that was actually run by two guys from Lahore. The spicy smell drifted in through the windows and made you hungry at inappropriate hours.

Dad had a job in IT that meant he worked when he liked, a fact I was pretty oblivious to until I started working. He had always been anti-establishment, always laughed at people who did the nine-to-five grind, pointing out the business types flocking to the station in their penguin suits as we drove past them on the way to school. Mom worked nine-to-five and I wonder now if that sort of stuff ever upset her. He'd been just as critical of my grandparents' traditions and their religion.

Nothing about him bothered me much when I lived with him after the divorce. Not even when he came stumbling back at three in the morning and woke me up playing The Dead Kennedys on the stereo during my GCSE exams.

Then he met this woman called Andrea. She didn't so much laugh at things as scream at them. She was always teasing Dad about his baldness, rubbing his head and making squeaky noises, calling him slaphead... I think she probably had her own issues because she had this face that didn't really move and these big fake boobs that she liked to show off in low-cut tops.

During my first year of sixth form, Dad and I had a massive falling out. I hadn't seen him for a week and when he finally came skulking home stinking of old beer and weed, he had a full head of hair. I say hair; it looked a bit like the wires on the end of a broom. The skin around his scalp was red. He'd also had something done to his eyes that made him look like he was walking into a hurricane. It felt like something tore inside me.

'It's just a bit of fun,' he said when I started having a go at him. When he smiled no crinkles appeared at his temples. 'What harm is it?'

'You looked fine before. Now you look weird,' I said in a high and shaky voice. 'You look like her.'

'Oh, I see. So that's what this is really about.'

I stormed out, and in a bit of a daze I ended up at Marlstone train station. It'd be another few years before I'd start getting the train to work from there, a few years before I'd start making up lives for that little bloke on the opposite platform. The trains to London flew past while the sun got steadily lower. The orange light from inside the carriages, all those blurred faces, were comforting to me. Perhaps I could be one of those people on the train.

After living with Dad I had a new-found respect for Mom. That's why I moved in with her. That, and the lack of other options.

I felt relieved when she shared with me all the reasons why she and Dad had split up (except on the odd occasion when the revelations veered a little too close to the bedroom). The first few months camped out in the downstairs bedroom of her house were really cathartic. He's selfish, he's dishonest, he's a womaniser. Yeah, yeah, and yeah. He bloody is.

She told me that on the night of their wedding he'd got so drunk he ended up having a pool game with his best mate Ron, and fell asleep in the bar of the hotel while she slept alone upstairs. About how she'd phoned him at a gig the night she'd gone into labour, and he'd gone on stage and done the show anyway, only arriving at the hospital two hours after I'd been born. He came in still talking about how well the gig had gone.

In turn I told her about all the inconsiderate things he'd done to me, although even as I said them I knew none of them had really bothered me as much as what he'd done with his hair.

Some nights she'd go on about him and it was like when she'd read me stories as a kid, when I'd never wanted the story to end because then she'd leave and I'd be alone. As one Dad-tale began to wind down, I'd grow tense, and then I'd grow immediately calm again when she'd say 'And don't get me started on...' and begin a new story.

For a while I saw my mom as the victim of my dad, of his charm and his energy. When he was younger he wasn't bad looking either and so I can see how she overlooked his complete lack of moral core. Like Dad, Mom came over to Britain with her parents as a baby. And like Dad she rejected lots of the traditional stuff that her parents believed. But unlike Dad, she still believed in things like being honest, and in the importance of family.

Thing is, I couldn't bring myself to dislike Dad. I just felt disappointed he wasn't as good as I'd thought he was. Mom hated that he wouldn't be what she wanted him to be, which I think is a different thing. The longer I lived with her, the more I wondered why my mom stayed with him for twenty years if he'd been so awful all this time. Where was her moral centre?

I woke up late one morning because I was on A-level study leave. Lying in the bath I could hear Mom on the phone to a friend, Lydia, in the study below. My mom hated Lydia, and went on to me about how she always had to drive Lydia around and how Lydia never understood what she was talking about because she hadn't got any GCSEs.

'I don't know what he plans to do,' I heard her say to Lydia. 'He can't keep staying here and living off me.' A pause. 'He leaves the dishes all over the place, spends all his time lying in bed.' A pause. 'No, never offers to help.' A pause. 'Exactly. Lazy. Like his dad. Lazy.' Another pause. 'And don't even get me started on that, don't even start me. He doesn't know the meaning of a job. If he wants to go to university he'll have to pay himself.'

Maybe if she'd have been cross with me when I went downstairs, things might have been okay between us. Instead, she smiled and asked me if I wanted a lift to college. No mention of the conversation with Lydia.

I doubt I'd have got brilliant exam results anyway, but I pretty much gave up on the idea of university at that point, so stopped putting in the effort. I'd been predicted an A in Music, and the teacher had told me that I should do this course in Guildford. I scraped a B and when I didn't mention uni to my parents they must have assumed I wasn't interested.

I needed to live in my own place and make my own money. I couldn't afford to move out straight away so I looked for work around Marlstone but nothing was going. The job centre found me work in Birmingham at an entertainment retailer that used to specialise in music before it decided it would try to sell everything and anything.

At the start I worked all the hours I could. It meant I was out of Mom's house, it meant I was saving more money, and I liked being at the train station every day. I felt connected to the world.

I also got to spend time with this girl who worked with me, Lola.

She sometimes worked mornings with me. She liked Queens of the Stone Age and all this other heavy music, and she had really cool opinions about stuff, like that democracy was all a big lie to make us think we're free, and that the media was full of shit trying to make people feel bad about the way they looked so they'd buy cosmetics to keep the economy going.

'You're smart like me, Parvez,' she said. 'You see things for what they are.'

She was hilarious with customers too, always slipping in sly little jokes that only I'd get, especially if they were wankers.

She started leaving me notes if we hadn't worked together for a while, telling me about things she'd done or stuff she'd thought up. Always on a folded up Post-it in my locker, always a little kiss at the end. Best of all she was from Marlstone, and hated it like I did.

Lola was pretty in this approachable, shabby sort of way. She had crooked fingernails, and the tip of one of her canines was black. I fancied her, but I couldn't tell if she liked me. She was always asking me about my old girlfriends and touching my hair, but then she was a couple of years older than me and probably had other boys her own age that she liked.

It didn't matter in the end. One morning I was telling her about London and she said, 'I might get out of here too. Getting a bit sick of what's going on in Marlstone.'

'What do you mean?' I said.

'Just mad, isn't it? How it's changing. We've just had another Paki family move over the road to us and my dad's thinking of selling up before the whole road gets taken over by them. Dad says it's devaluing the area.'

I didn't know what to say to her. I said nothing and tried to keep the anger off my face. Later, when she'd gone, I went to the toilet and looked in the mirror to double-check my skin colour. I'm not even joking.

After that I spent less time working than I wanted to, and I tried to avoid Lola as much as I could. My savings were looking pretty healthy by then.

I started thinking the problem was deep: like, what even is a person? Maybe it's different to being like a train or a guitar. Maybe when you experience what you think is a person, it's a bit like seeing faces and patterns in the stars at night. You see someone saying all this stuff they believe and hope and dream, but really it's you linking it all together to make a single thing called Mom or Dad or Lola. It's just a game of join the dots but with no rules, no different to what I was doing inventing lives for my skinny friend at the train station.

One morning Iggy Pop was on the telly trying to sell me insurance. I was trying to eat my breakfast. I'd been listening to Iggy since before sixth form, since before my parents split up. One hot, windless summer of mock-exam stress I listened to Iggy every night to help me sleep.

I don't know why, but it was worse than all of the rest. Worse than Dad, and Mom, and Lola. If Iggy's for sale then what's the point of anything?

I went to work that day listening to The Ramones. I thought old music was better because those people didn't try very hard to be liked. Today all I see is old men and old women trying to impress young people, like young people know what the fuck they're doing. We don't know what we're doing. We need help.

At the train station I watched my friend on the other side of the platform. I was still furious with Iggy and the world. One of the high-speed trains that doesn't stop at Marlstone roared towards us, London bound, and the little bloke opposite barely flinched on his bench. He was lost in his thoughts. But I didn't start fantasising about him like usual. I was too down.

I should have been inspired. I'd been waiting for just the right disappointment to motivate me across the bridge to the opposite platform, but if the Iggy thing wasn't going to do it what would?

I doubted myself. Did I really want to go to London? What was stopping me?

I got on the train to work, to Birmingham, and considered that maybe disappointment just wasn't a very good motivator.

Then I decided the truth was I didn't have the balls. Ultimately, I was still too Marlstone.

Then one day, my skinny friend changed everything for me. I remember there was a slight breeze that morning, because the little wave of greying blond hair was flapping up and down on the top of his head. The train station was quieter than usual because I'd missed my train. And from the look of it, he had missed his.

He looked more thoughtful than usual. I didn't think much of it. I did think about how coincidental it was that we'd both missed a train that morning, but it didn't occur to me until later that I'd never actually seen him get on a train to London, and that perhaps it was just one more of the many things I'd invented about him.

From my right, I heard the distant beeping of road barriers coming down to indicate the approach of a high-speed train. I looked up at the bridge over the tracks. Someone had recently painted EDL on the side in yellow.

'Mate, what the fuck are you doing?' a man shouted. My skinny friend was no longer on his bench. He was down on the train tracks, briefcase in hand. 'There's a train coming!'

My friend didn't react. The expression on his face was the same one I'd seen every day, thoughtful, slightly nervous, determined.

The train came around the corner from the left, growing larger even in the fraction of a second my eyes dwelled on it. Someone else was yelling, and then another person, panic spreading as my friend knelt down in the middle of the tracks facing the approaching train. I got to my feet.

The *chhhhh* of metal on metal rose to drown out all the shouting, while my own cry was blocked by my thumping heart.

All the while my friend went on with his business. He placed the briefcase down in front of him, put his hands together, then as the train approached put his head forward just very slightly.

I imagine people screamed and shouted, although I was silent. Nothing was audible over the sound of the train braking.

The horn blared.

He was there, then he wasn't.

By the time the train stopped, it was much further down the tracks. It eventually reversed a little so that those on board could step off if they wanted to.

It all happened so quickly that I'll never really know if I actually saw my friend smile before the train hit him. The corner of his mouth just moving up very slightly at the same moment he closed his eyes.

In retrospect, the atmosphere after the crash was upsettingly calm, although I didn't actually get upset until later. At the time it felt normal, like I just needed to come up with another little story about my friend and what he'd done.

Was it cowardly to do something like that? To finish things rather than deal with your problems? Or was it an act of great courage? Overcoming the instinct for survival and putting an end to your own suffering for good. Either way, it didn't matter to me. Both acts were so decisive and so deliberate, that I couldn't help feeling inspired. Although that doesn't feel like quite the right word.

I climbed up the stairs of the bridge. Up on top I saw a few people coming towards me, people who'd left the train in search of another route. London people: they don't like delays. Each one stepped around some dark object resting on the walkway. When I got close enough I was relieved to see it was just the top corner of a briefcase, the exposed wood poking out from beneath the torn leather like a bone. That was it for remains. Even when I got to the other side and climbed aboard the train I didn't see anything. Like he'd been a cartoon person.

Some passengers were still on board. I imagined they must have experienced something like it before, the way they were acting. I sat down behind a man talking on his phone and typing on his laptop.

'Yeah, we're stuck in somewhere called Marlstone,' the man said. 'With any luck not for much longer.'

This new story from Matthew Licht is a companion piece to 'Across the Kinderhook', which appeared in our anthology Crying Just Like Anybody.

Mental Pictures

Matthew Licht

Me and Jilly went through a rough patch in November. More impenetrable than rough, really. In other words, we didn't make it through, or not together. In October, I had most of the basic civilised person requisites, like a job, place to live, some friends, and a good woman by my side. Then the world went cold and it started to rain a lot and I got, in short order, fired, lonely, and propelled into the cheap rental apartment market.

Twenty years in the same pad adds up to a mound of heartbreaking accumulated crap, pulled out of the communal closet and spilled on the floor. Used to be fun, going out to hunt for stuff we thought we needed or wanted. Can't split a cast-iron

Dutch oven, when the yelling and crying's over. Can't split anything, really, except a couple that seemed like a solid bet for eternity. After a look at the roomful of clutter I said keep whatever you want, baby, tell the Salvation Army to come for the rest. Then I was out the door and didn't know where I was headed, except maybe to the park for a wandering howl in the rain. Which is where I went and what I did.

The city went dark in a hurry. The concept of no place to go sunk in like lightning, then the rain picked up the insane pace. The park is no place for a civilised person to live. You have to de-civilise yourself to survive there. The process takes time and effort.

The bus station wasn't crowded. The patient lady in the ticket booth read me the schedule for buses to Scranton a few times. The mental patient before her couldn't absorb the numbers, didn't really want to return to the haystacks and move back in with his mother as a forty-seven-year-old unemployed newly single social reject. But that was reality, perfect splendid brutal and honest.

The obsolete-looking bus named Scranton groaned in recognition as I boarded. The suspension didn't suspend judgment. Home goes the loser. Maybe it was the same bus I got on the last time I lost my mind, when I decided to go to college in the big city instead of giving my old man a hand in the garage so I could eventually take over, the way he wanted and the way I wanted too, for a while. Stuff you thought you wanted changes, or moves on to hang out among the possible pasts and futures you missed or avoided, until you don't want what you thought you wanted anymore. I didn't want to go back home and the past possible future no longer existed. Pop's garage had been sold and turned into a fast food joint. In other words, a place where they *might* offer me a job. Mama still lived in the house we called home. The place was the same as it always was, last time

I'd looked, except she didn't take such good care of it anymore. Maybe she never took care of the place, only I didn't use to know any different. She didn't get out too often either — not that she went out terribly often when Pop was still around — on account of she had a major stroke after too many years of drinking too much.

Alcoholism runs in families, like baldness, cancer, red hair, amyotrophic lateral sclerosis. I don't consider myself an alcoholic. I was on my way back to Scranton.

The outdated bus filled up quickly, as the scheduled departure Zero Hour loomed. With only minutes to go, I was the only damp, sour-smelling, lonely-vibe-emanating loser with a free seat next to him. Would've been happy about this state of affairs at any other time, but additional leper status was upsetting. I was still in New York, technically. Hadn't officially gone back to Scranton to live with my mother yet. And even then, it was only until I found a job and another place to live. I figured I could write off the 'good woman by my side and friends' clause of the social contract. Found out pretty quickly how many friends I really had, when the trouble started.

'Is this seat free, please, sir?'

Smoked voice snapped me out of a blank-eyed, open-mouthed reverie that could've turned into another howl-a-thon any second. 'Sure,' I said. 'Free as a bird.' As if birds are really free.

But there were two people in the bus aisle ogling the empty seat next to the empty-lived reluctant one-way passenger to Palookaville, USA. A big-boned blonde a shade past her expiration date on the dish register and a kid who looked disturbingly like me.

Like me the way I looked at that moment, I mean. Not how I looked when I was a kid. So the blowsy babe didn't say, 'Remember that drunken car-hump where you said you were totally sure you pulled out all the way at the last second? Well you was wrong, buster. Looks like your lone one-night-stand infidelity rampage just caught up with you.' Instead, she said, 'Go ahead and sit down next to the nice man, Adam.'

Adam sat down. No point asking if he wanted the window seat. Any seat was fine and the same, to him. He had Down's syndrome and it was awful dark out there anyhow.

'He has a tendency to become extremely nervous on buses, kind sir. Would you mind checking on him occasionally? All you have to do is ask whether he's okay. That's usually enough to reassure him. And maybe accompany him to the restroom, please, if he gets carsick. Although he's been better about that lately.'

'Oh sure. No problem. But... you mean, you're not coming with him?'

'He's going to stay with his father a while. We're divorced. This is what we agreed on so we don't have to see each other. But if you'd rather not...'

Adam looked at me. Would've taken a hard guy to say get your stinking mongoloid out of my face, lady. And I was nothing but a lump of bacon grease left on a radiator and illuminated by dust-sparkled sunbeams in a depressing but cheap studio apartment in Hell's Kitchen.

The lady didn't say goodbye honey or bon voyage, see you next week. She spun on her heavy-duty medium-high heel and walked down the bus aisle without a backward glance or a word to the driver, who was busy adjusting his super-professional driving gloves.

As soon as she got off, he started the motor and pulled the anachronistic door-close lever.

Adam the abnormal kid wanted to hold hands as the bus exited the Port of Authority at a dizzying eight miles per hour. Gave a sad moan and closed his eyes when it hit the ramp that led down into the Tunnel of Sheer Shaking Terror. The Expressway tollbooth frightened him too, even though the nice man who collected tolls shouted good evening everybody, which was his human way of dealing with an inhuman job.

Adam resumed normal snuffle-breathing when we were on the highway headed west.

'Thanks,' he said, and pulled his dry hand from mine. He soon fell asleep, with his forehead pressed against the quilted steel seat-back ahead of him. Lights from motels, gas stations, billboards, diners, cars headed into town, and trucks hauling breakfast materials so the big city could get a good start on the next workday played against the pale blank screen of Adam's left profile.

Couldn't sleep. The black window reflected a scared sad luck-lost straggler headed nowhere good at a rock-steady fifty-five miles per hour. So I stared uselessly out the front window, where the driver was looking, to make sure he was still awake and doing his job properly. He was fine. He was on schedule and in control. Highway signs hypnotised me into a dream-free oblivion.

It was still dark when we hit Scranton. Rolled past the high school, the church where I used to pretend to pray. When I confessed, my mother said she was just pretending too, but that pretending religion was okay. Pop the Pragmatic Mechanic didn't go to church, didn't believe and didn't want to pretend there was more to life and the world than what's visible in broad daylight. The bus went down Skid Row at a solemn pace, turned left towards the granite Deco-Fascist terminal. Tried to pretend there was something pleasant about a return to a familiar place.

'Wake up, Adam. We're here. Need to go to the bathroom?'

Adam said he did indeed need to use the bathroom. So I waited, sort of glad he could handle liquid waste elimination on his own and that he hadn't vomited or drooled on me. Glad to be glad about something. I tried to figure out how old he was, gave up. Definitely over fourteen, probably not yet thirty. A few white hairs on the back of his neck, but that might be part of the syndrome, not necessarily significant.

The driver found his designated berth, parked, switched off the engine, and started rubbing his eyes obsessively, like he couldn't bear to watch the somnolent hulks and husks behind him stir to life, grab their crapsacks from the overhead compartments where endless other burdens had been stowed, and skulk off his vehicle. The aisle was soon clear.

Adam was stuck in the toilet. He rattled the latch, increasingly frantic, then pounded on the door, burbling, about to scream and cry. I stood up and stumbled to the back, unsure whether to talk him down from the outside or hustle towards the front to get a hypothetical toilet-lock override key from the haggard driver, who wanted nothing more than an empty bus so he could get off and take a leak in the employee men's room, get coffee and breakfast, then either crash in the bus company's employee lodgings, or take a short nap and pull a double shift, make the return haul back to wherever he lived. I imagined a Long Island suburb for the guy, a place like Babylon, Bay Shore, or Northport. Saw the wonderful white windswept beach where Jilly and I used to go and be happy together. She borrowed a shack, a former chicken coop in some fisher-family's back yard, rented by a lesbian chick she worked with, an admirer who was always sincerely glad to do Jilly a favour. Nice break from the city, job, and cramped studio pad. A chicken coop felt palatial.

The gay lady at Jilly's ad agency was probably glad her not-so-secret crush had finally gotten over her straight shack-job phase and was ready to move on, spread out, explore.

The driver heard Adam's bestial confused terror, grasped the situation immediately and took charge. He scrambled the emergency key, held it out on a golden beam of sympathetic solidarity. Maybe he had an idiot kid stashed in Paramus, Union, or Hoboken.

'Cool down, Adam,' I said. 'We'll get you out of there in a minute.'

There was no lone adult male waiting on the platform, ready to rush in and rescue his not-quite-right kid, whose fears, limitations, and difficulties he knew intimately, from the claustrophobic bus toilet.

Adam emerged drawn, gaunt even though he was on the chubby side, pale as a dirty pillowcase. He grabbed for an instinctual hug. I swung him side-to-side in a go-nowhere slow dance, patted his slack back, and said everything was all right. Heard Jilly's voice in my head. 'See? You can do the normal human stuff if you stop being afraid for a hot minute. The feelings and abilities are imprinted on your DNA. All you have to do is let them out, let them go.' But it was too late and I was still totally terrified of the warm natural things that Nature hands out free so life can go on, for whatever reason it does, and be bearable because you got some happy memories and maybe you were of some use to someone, once. Gave another, younger person life, a place to live, food to eat, possible explanations for inexplicable mysteries, maybe a good example of how to live for when you're gone and they're on their own.

'Let's go, Adam. Let's get off so the nice driver can finish what he needs to do. Where are you supposed to meet your father?'

Another lost look.

We headed down the aisle holding hands in a two-man Dance of Death where I was the bad guy. 'He's probably waiting inside the terminal, where it's warmer.'

'Have a nice day,' the driver said. He thumped Adam's narrow sloping shoulder and handed him an official bus company corporate logo pin, a streamlined chrome racing mutt to wear on his jacket so he could pretend he was a big strong bus driver too. I loved the bus driver.

Possible career opportunity, I thought, if only I could force myself to be strong, steadfast and true. Maybe Greyhound's like the Army or the Foreign Legion, a place where they have to take a man in and give him something to do, as long as he's got two legs, arms, eyes, and brain cells to rub together.

'Thanks,' I said. 'Really appreciate it.'

Adam said the same, imitating my voice, including the sentimental catch. On the platform, he wanted me to pin on his bus driver badge for him. I jabbed my finger with it.

The sprawling poorly maintained lobby contained some obvious hobos contortion-crashed out on the bolted-down benches, a few lost-looking ladies, and men in car coats and heavy-weather headgear, perhaps in the first phases of hunting expeditions or fishing trips. Or off to football games at their far-flung Alma Maters. Or on fraught odysseys to get problematic sons out of jail, attend trials for murder, mayhem, grand theft auto. The men weren't bus drivers, in any case. And none of them was Adam's father.

I pictured a guy on the delinquent side, someone Adam's big blonde mommy-lady would get hot for in a flash and get tired of a bit slower, as rock'n'roll family fantasies skidded from the East Village to a trailer park near a raceway on the outskirts of some dog-dick South Jersey beach town.

'What's your father look like, Adam?'

He had to think about it. A blurred image-bank scrolled behind his soft-focus milky blue eyes. Men previously seen, important and less so. For the moment, I was in the fairly important category. Or else I was only fooling myself that I could interpret mongoloid thought-processes.

'Kind of like me,' he said. 'Only bigger.' Adam had a sense of humour, or we were looking for a Pilt-Down's Syndrome Man who beat the sterility stipulation in the extra-chromosome natural selection deal. We ambled around the Scranton Terminal. The newsstand was either still closed, or closed for good.

No one was expecting me. I hadn't called to let my mother know I was on my way. Couldn't force my stupid mouth to form the loser mantra. Had to force my hands into my pockets to pull out soaked crumpled bills to pay for the bus ticket. Pretended some shadowy being had a gun trained on my spinal cord when I boarded.

No one was waiting for Adam, either. Congenital defect daddy-o had skipped out on civilised responsibility, skipped town when the broad he'd knocked up and wouldn't leave him alone had called and said, 'Listen I need a break because I might be onto something good with this older guy I met. I've kept the punk two years now. A month or two is alls I need and then you can re-deliver. If I get set up right... and I got a feeling this could be it... I already told him about Adam, honest... then you and me don't never need to lay eyes on each other again.'

The last idea had definite appeal. But Adam's pop might not have believed the party of the first part. All the parties were over, as far as Adam's mom and pop were concerned. The parties shut down the minute he was born. Might've been that way even if he'd turned out right, who knows?

'Here's what we do, Adam,' I said. 'Let's go to *my* mommy's house and wait for your daddy there. Unless you want to have breakfast here first.'

'Breakfast here first.'

That's what I wanted, too. Extra hour or so in the terminal diner to gear up for the impending inevitable. And it wasn't impossible that some past-it hood would turn up, plead engine trouble and take Adam off my hands.

Wasn't in me to take the case to the cops. Even if I knew cops was the best idea, in this case. They'd probably take my number and address, ask some questions, eventually bring Adam back and say, 'Listen mister, do you mind? Poor kid's got nowhere else to go, for the moment, and we sorta got more important, police-type business to worry about.'

'What's your mother look like?' Adam asked, after the waitress took our order.

Since he was so curious, I gave it to him straight, no details spared. Veiny eyeballs, tongue like a bad stretch of cracked pink pavement, front teeth with blackened seams across the middle, crowned by Dr Spannick the cut-rate dentist with the hairy hands and horrible breath. The thought of giving my mother a kiss hello gave me pause over a plate of corned beef hash with fried eggs and ketchup. So I thought about what it'd be like to kiss Adam's mother instead.

'Hey Adam, what's your phone number? We should call your mom to let her know we got here and you're okay.'

He shook his head hard enough to dislodge the glasses from behind a round, banal ear.

'What? You don't know your own home number?'

He choked a snigger like maybe he knew but wasn't about to tell.

'Don't you have it written down somewhere? Like in your pocket, in case you get lost? This is kind of important, Adam. Do you want your nice mommy to worry about you?' Mental note to stop talking to the poor kid like he was an idiot. Talk normal to him, stupid. What's wrong with you? No one likes to be patronised by relative strangers who aren't relatives and have nothing to be high and mighty about.

'More about your mother. More about your mother,' Adam said, like my mother was some unbelievably humorous comic book character, on the order of Fartman, about whom an infinite series of dirty-joke-like adventures can be told when laughter's the only face to put on a situation.

'Okay I forgot to tell you... her face is burning red. Especially when she gets angry, and you got to watch your step around her, 'cause she gets angry real easy. For instance, suppose I was to go like this...' Hoisted a butt cheek and let go a post-bus decompression fart.

Comic genius slays mentally retarded male of indeterminate age.

'Oh man she'd blow a gasket. You know what she'd probably do? Spank me, that's what. Spank me with a shovel... a god damn *snow* shovel.'

A glance out the window showed it had started snowing, in a weepy sort of way. Eight o'clock in the morning. My mother probably wasn't awake yet, wouldn't be too thrilled about being disturbed for another hour or so.

Pictured Jilly getting ready to go to work, her first day as the newly single creative director at a major ad agency, a hot commodity on the swinging corporate-world market. Cup of strong coffee and *The New Yorker*, this week's or a back issue. The subscription label still had my name on it. Jilly in pyjama bottoms and a hooded sweatshirt. Basically doing fine, maybe glad for enhanced closet space and one less depressed person in the pad. Nearly went off on another weeping jag, but I was in the middle of telling a mentally handicapped person a funny story about my mother. Kept scanning the parking lot outside the Terminal Diner. Maybe the creep who sired Adam would still show up. I could try to stick him with the breakfast check.

'... and then she jammed her butt-picking fingers in my nose, like this.' Self-inflicted nostril-grab. 'And dragged me over barbed wire and broken glass. And then she made me eat a rat. Didn't even cook it first. But that was okay, 'cause she's a lousy cook. She's awful mean, Adam. But only with me. She'll be nice to you. You guys'll be best friends, I guarantee it.' Like he'd already moved in.

The early morning waitress patted Adam's head and said whenever he wanted to come back and visit, she'd give him a free slice of yesterday's peach pie. There's always a piece of yesterday's pie left over, for nice guys. She barely looked at me, even though I left her a better than decent tip. Maybe she could tell what happened, what I did, even though I was pretending to be the funny-looking kid's responsible pseudo-pop. I ditched my common-law wife because I couldn't stand the way our life together was headed. I was a creep. I bore the mark of creepy loserdom.

We left the bus station on foot. Adam took my hand at the crosswalks, dropped it the instant we were safely across. Mrs Rosscom was opening up the Smoke'n'Novelty Shop her crazy husband had dumped on her when The Reaper socked him a one-two punch of emphysema and liver cancer. Left his widow with two hundred square yards of downtown commercial space jammed to the bulging eyeballs with practical joke items, tobacco-related paraphernalia, backdated cheesecake mags and selected hardcore stuff racked in pressboard shelves in the northwest corner, where a two-foot-tall red-green macaw named Ixnay blew an air raid siren at shoplifters and scattered approximately three dollars of bird seed on the floor every ding-dong day.

Mrs Rosscom pegged me instantly. Mert's punk kid, who once stole thirty-five cents' worth of candy bracelets. I wanted to give them cute little Shirley Stevens, first big love of my life, who never even looked at me because she was in seventh grade and I was in fifth. An incorrigible repeat offender, I rolled up a war-horror comic and stuck it down the front of my pants like no one would notice a John Holmes boner on an eleven-year-old. Her look now said see, you eventually have to pay for your crimes and sins. You had high-flown dreams of success in the big city, college boy, but you got stuck with a life-crushing millstone around your neck too. Your genes are defective. Look at the monster your love and loins produced. Welcome back to Scranton. Did you really think you could get away?

'Hey Teeter, what's shakin'?' The answer was her hands, in the primary stages of Parkinson's disease. Teeter was Mrs Rosscom's nickname in high school. My mother Mert still called her that, even though she didn't like it. Or maybe *because* she didn't like it. My mom got stuck with Mert, because Myrtle was a popular name, a long time ago. I didn't know what Teeter Rosscom's real name was, and right then I didn't care.

She didn't even hear me. She was too wrapped up in giving Adam a third-degree love mugging.

'You and your daddy are in town to visit grammy Mert, huh?' Mental logic counters chugged to calculate why we might be there in the middle of the week with no major holidays in sight. 'Why I'd bet a hunnerd bucks it's your birthday, big boy, so I'm gonna give you a present. Come on inside.'

Candy bracelets had rocketed to a nickel apiece. Adam emerged like a millionaire matron exiting Tiffany's, admiring his new chiclet ice at arm's length, with a small-town swinger mag tucked under his flaccid armpit.

'Thanks a lot, Teeter.'

'Tell Mert I said hi. Wanna bring her some smokes? You know, she has trouble getting down here these days and I need the business more than the superdupermarket does.'

'Sure. Give me two cartons of Kools and a joy buzzer.'

'You'd love to give her a heart attack on top of it, wouldn't you. Finish the job.'

'Okay. Screw you and keep your stale coffin nails.'

Teeter decided I wasn't worth looking at any more. She beamed on Adam again. 'Well at least you're a nice young man, young fella whatever-your-name-is. Come back to the store and I'll give you another present and then we'll watch football or whatever you like and you can tell me all about yourself.'

Mert wasn't awake yet and I didn't have keys to the house I grew up in. Hand 'em over, college boy. We'll have to take in boarders if you won't lend a hand.

Hopes and dreams landed me a gig at the Museum of Modern Art when my career as an art mover was played out. Couldn't face blister-wrap, packer's tape and clear pine splinters any more, or the abstract millions being shuttled around for the benefit of people I rarely saw. Worked a connection with a chick I knew in college. She wanted to be Sylvia Plath, only alive and not nuts, but she settled for running a museum book-and-gift shop. She got me in.

Selling tickets wasn't too dismal. Some human contact, at least. And I could let my friends into the museum for free, except they stopped coming around. Seemed like they were embarrassed.

Jilly made a career leap, from hand and foot model to advertising agent. She never said she was disappointed in me.

Would she let me back into our insufficient but cheap Hell's Kitchen pad? Could I cross that dingy threshold again without splitting into dissatisfied atoms?

Or bring Adam back to the city, locate and return him to his stacked blonde mom who could've had a career in Smoke'n'Joke-style men's mags. Maybe that's what she did to stay alive, in real life. She looked vaguely, if not *Vogue*-ly, familiar. Tried to re-conjure her cover-girl image while I worked up the resolve to pound on the brown chipped-paint door so the sickly crone inside would return to conscious life and let me in where it was warm.

What kind of woman would put her retarded kid on a bus alone when she knew the guy who was supposed to be on the receiving end had a history of being somewhat unreliable? Or maybe the plan was more like shuffle the idiot burden who's dragging me down over to the station, put him on the next bus leaving town and spot a sucker who looks like he'll look after him when he realises he's been stuck with a package of destiny.

The rule for gamblers with fundamental smarts is, if you can't figure out who the sucker in the poker game is, then the sucker is you. This counts as self-realisation. Take yourself politely out of the game before the next crooked hand is dealt, sucker.

The door opened a crack to reveal a red eyeball buried among wrinkles and a row of brown teeth with barn-door gaps between them. 'Whadduya want?'

But I was sure she recognised me.

'How 'bout letting us in, Mert?' I stopped calling her Maw even before I started shaving. 'Kinda cold out here.'

She took the chain off. Background squalor popped into view. 'So... college boy. 'Bout time you paid a visit. Too bad your pop's not around for this honour. He died, you know?'

'I was at the funeral, Mert.' Adam needed a slight shove between the kidneys to get him going inside. Maybe Mert's place smelled like the scary bus toilet.

'Where's your snooty girlfriend? Who's this kid? Don't tell me...'

'Not what you think, Mert. Whatever you're thinking.' Got Adam's jacket off. His sexy negligent mom didn't even put a hat on his head. His hair was even thinner at the top. 'Adam here got a little lost, but we'll have him straightened out soon. Right now he'd probably like to take a nap, because it was a lo-ong bus ride. You feel like taking a nap, Adam?'

'Maybe later. Can I go to the toilet?'

Mert grabbed his pudgy hand. 'I'll take you, honey. While this galoot makes a pot of coffee.' Unsuspected maternal instincts had been aroused. She guided him upstairs. Maybe she'd give him a bath. Maybe she'd take one herself. Eye-popping picture of Adam's mom in a bathtub, her coral-pink nipples bobbing in heavenly foam.

The kitchen was brute-filthy. Set some water to boil and cleaned up a bit. Shades of my early days as a dishwasher in an Upper Broadway jazz joint where they slung burgers and chilli, a place where other college students hung out. And some of them really did snap their fingers. But at least they didn't snap their fingers at me. 'Hey boy get these congealed-ketchup plates out of our way so we can pretend to be soulful, here.'

Didn't get fired, there. Just didn't show up one day. Couldn't stand to hear Freddie Freeloader or So What even one more time. Informal contracts get broken when the breaking point's reached, including those that govern love.

Felt good to wash dishes again. Mopped the kitchen linoleum. Got out the vacuum cleaner, a bulbous sci-fi robot model, and gave the living room shabbery a going-over. Watery sound waves descended. Old Mert really *was* giving Adam a bath and a back-scrub. Maybe the first since his baby days. Adam's amscray mama didn't exactly seem like an attention- and physical maintenance-lavishing kind of lady. But then, neither did Mert. Adam's skin was awful dry. Maybe Mert used to stash bottom-drawer gin behind moisturising lotion in the medicine cabinet. She would've killed me if she'd ever caught me illegally using any of her beauty goop, and Pop would've thought I was a homo.

Framed photo of an old car Pop thought particularly snazzy next to an autographed Liberace headshot on the living room wall. Took them off their hooks, dusted the gilt, spritzed the house's last few drops of Windex on the glass.

Mert was reading Adam a rhyming story that sounded incredibly like *Horatius at the Bridge*. Either Mert had poetry tomes secreted in her room, or she knew those verses by heart. Both concepts blew my mind. Brain-atoms skittered across the universe at light-speed. Didn't want to look in, interrupt, and break the spell.

Strayed into my mind that Adam must know his sexy mom's name, even if telephone numbers were a problem. There's still such a thing as directory assistance, though it's no longer a toll-free call. Used to dial 411 just to hear a human voice, usually a black lady's. I'd make up names to find out if certain imaginary persons actually existed in the Manhatto-sphere. Sometimes I gave my own name, just to hear there was no such party listed, therefore I didn't existed. Got an idea Adam's mom's name was Debbie, maybe because she reminded me of a chick who used to get in a lot of trouble for smoking in the girls' room at school. Debbie Spinello's pop, the town barber, was gunned down under mysterious circumstances.

Maybe Debbie Spinello moved to the big city, got knocked up by a party or parties unknown and gave live birth to a kid who didn't turn out as planned or unplanned.

Mert was reading Victorian epic poetry to a mongoloid. Anything was possible.

Debbie Spinello and I had groped our way through a short string of sweaty car dates. Since my pop was a mechanic, at least I always had a car. He sold me a long string of lemons before I got wise. High school jocks called car dates with Debbie 'goin' for a Spin.' Took a while, but I got to the point where I wasn't jealous. Long-dormant busted-rubber blues nightmares played in my head. But the dates didn't match up, no matter how I scrambled and cooked the books. Maybe Adam was older than he looked. See if I could get him to tell me his true age without blowing a brain valve.

Mert stuck her head in the door and burst yet another reverie. 'What a sweet little guy. How come you never had any kids, college boy? Probably too late now.'

'Definitely too late, Mert. Forgot to tell you... Jilly and I aren't together any more. Drifted apart, like in that Elvis song you used to sing along with, and broke up. But don't worry. She's got a great job, she can afford the rent and she likes city life.'

'Not her I'm worried about. She's the kind who knows how to look out for herself. But what're you gonna do? Open a home for lost retards? Can't do it here, I tell you that right now.'

'One step at a time, Mert. I thought I'd look after you a while, but you seem to have regained your snap.'

'You always were too-little-too-late. But I appreciate it... and I heard they're looking for someone to load the dishwasher at the Terminal Diner.'

'Fantastic. I'll go apply first thing tomorrow.' I meant it, too. The thought of a modest salary, free grub, and maybe discount-rate lodging at the Bus Terminal Hotel had immediate visceral appeal. I wanted the job, even if I had to wrestle someone for it, even an alligator. Hadn't felt that way in a long time. 'Thanks, Mert.'

'How come you stopped calling me Mama? You used to, once.'

'When I grew up you just seemed more like Mert, that's all. What's Adam doing?'

'Taking a nap. He asked if the story about Horatius was true. I think he would've dropped off sooner if I said it was just a story.'

'How come you never read me any poems, Mert?'

'Don't blame me, blame your old man. I wanted to, but he said it'd turn you into a sissy. Really finished him, when you went away and didn't want to take over his business. And he thought it was my fault you left, too.'

'I lost all curiosity about how or why other people's cars work or don't work. And then I didn't feel like fixing them when they stopped.'

'Story of your life.'

'And a true one.'

'You always wanted to know if the stories in books from the library were real. But I wasn't lying. They're probably based on stuff that really happened. Most stories start out that way, even if they're not true like stuff in newspapers.'

'Newspaper stories aren't true either, Mert. I worked at a paper for a while. Stories come in one way and go out another.' Best job I ever had, in terms of dough. Memories of loathsome reporters and editors flitted. Dishwashing was a relative picnic and kite-flying contest.

At home, me and Jilly took turns making dinner and cleaning up. The kitchen in our pad was too small for two people to do such normal everyday things together. Some friends who lived in Jersey had two bathrooms in their ranch-moderne house, with two sinks apiece. Blew my mind there were still people who actually managed to live that way. Broke my heart that Jilly and I couldn't figure out how. We nearly split up over a choice of fabric to reupholster an Arts and Crafts cabin sofa we bought from a toothless lesbian speed-freak couple at the sixth Avenue flea market. Couldn't even figure out something as simple as that, towards the end.

Mert used to take care of home-front details. Pop sat on the couch in grease-stained overalls until dinner time. Mert either didn't care or didn't have the gumption to leave. Her high school portraits spelled out that she was never much to look at. Maybe she made up for it by being a mattress-back, like Debbie Spinello. Maybe Pop had a shotgun pointed at his sacral iliac when he said I do and I will. Rows upon rows of shotguns and deer-hunting rifles packed the racks at Mossberger's Sporting Goods on Main Street. The place had closed down, but some mysterious party or parties kept the pink neon sign buzzing at night. Seemed like a weirdo colour scheme for a store whose stock-in-trade was animal death. Pink foam bubbled from the snouts of lung-shot stags tied to auto fenders while the heroes celebrated their tribal meat conquests with beer in the Flame Tavern.

One staggering dickhead said you got to love the animals before you kill them. That's the spirit of hunting, he said. Love.

At least I never killed an animal. In that way, I'm at peace. A guy I worked with at the art-movers company fell asleep at the wheel on a Dallas run, rammed a car headed north. The victim driver lost a leg. My colleague couldn't live with what he did, even though the injured party said hey accidents happen, I'm glad I'm still alive and now, though disabled, I'll be able to spend more time with my kids. My colleague got himself ancestored into a merchant seaman gig, on the Taiwan route. Never saw him again, which is probably how he wanted it. The accident turned me into one of the ghosts he didn't want to see.

'Got anything to make lunch with, Mert?'

'Not unless you want cheese and crackers, or crackers and sardines.'

'Lend me the car. I'll go to the supermarket.'

'Sold it. DMV says I can't drive any more on account of my eyes are bad and I got some trouble moving the left side of my carcass because I had a major stroke, in case you forgot.'

Hadn't noticed the missing Oldsmobile in the abbreviated driveway in front of the ramshackle garage, maybe because I didn't want to see my old man's lovingly maintained now-crumbling dreamboat turned mechanical memento mori. A look out the window confirmed that the dead car was gone. But the sorry sight-that-wasn't was still burned on my cerebral cortex.

Waited for Adam to finish his nap before I went shopping. Maybe the friendly butcher would toss us an extra turkey drumstick or a free pound of high-fat hamburger if Adam smiled and said hi. Maybe the cash register chick would forget to charge us for ice cream and frozen pie.

At around one-thirty, I couldn't wait any longer. The kid was a prodigious napper. Got to be good at something. Had to shake him pretty hard. Worried me, for a minute or two. Then his inexpressive eyes opened to full dullness.

'C'mon. I need a big strong guy to help carry stuff from the supermarket. You ready?'

'Yeah.'

Mongoloids, like orang-utans, are supposedly endowed with superhuman strength. They draw on power reserves which more fortunate humans keep under emergency brake, for use in extreme situations. Hero mom catches sixteen-ton safe before it crushes her baby carriage. Fired postal clerk massacres fifty former co-workers with his bare hands. Adam could probably grab my ankles and tear me in half, if he felt like it, but he let me hold his hand all the way to the supermarket. The streets of Scranton were still strange to him, after all. Strange to me, again.

'Is your mother's name Debbie, Adam? Or Deborah... or Deb, something like that?'

'Nope.' He shook his head vigorously at the mere thought.

'Okay, what *is* her name, then?'

'Uhm... forgot.'

'Come on, Adam. No one forgets his own mommy's name. What's *my* mommy's name?'

He looked at me like that was a real dumb question. 'Mert. Only she's not mean, like you said.'

'I said she was only mean to me. But you're right. All that meanie stuff was just a story I made up 'cause I thought it was funny... to make you laugh, get it? But good jokes are usually on the short side. Tell me your mommy's name so we can look for her and get you back home.'

'Forgot.' He pulled my hand so I'd lean down. Then he whispered a secret. 'She said to say I forgot. But I really remember.'

'You can tell me, Adam. I won't tell her you didn't do what she said.'

He shook his head hard, pulled me lower. 'She said she wouldn't love me any more if I told anyone her name.'

His insufficient brain was primed to explode. Bad as old Mert could sometimes be, she never said she wouldn't love me if I got kicked out of school again, or if the cops brought me home drunk and disorderly again, or if I got another girl pregnant so she had to go away to the unwed mothers' home in Keekatchie. 'Don't worry, Adam. Your mommy loves you an awful lot. You know that, don't you?'

Dull ray of sweet hope dawned. Another vigorous, positive head-wag.

'Only she's in some kind of trouble. That's why she put you with me for a while. We can help her out by staying calm. But right now let's help my mean old mommy Mert by going to the supermarket for ice cream and a birthday cake. Because I got a feeling someone's got a birthday coming up soon. Am I right?'

He thought I might be trying to trick him. 'Maybe.'

'Look, there's no law says it's got to be your real birthday when you buy a birthday cake. Today's the day we get to do whatever we want. After we get back from the supermarket, that is.'

Mrs Abernathy ran the supermarket bakery. She said since Adam's cake was a special order, he had to put the icing on himself. She taught him how to ice cakes without making a mess and made sure he spelled his name right. Mr Klottke the butcher insisted, when he heard hamburgers royale were on the late-lunch menu, that we take an extra pound of top ground sirloin, just in case he decided to show up for the party. Then he threw in a bottle of his home-brew steak sauce, inscribed 'No Charge, for Adam's Birthday'. The cash register chick said ice cream was on special half-price sale, only the lazy stockboys hadn't put up the colourful signs and balloons yet.

She winked at Adam. 'Don't tell anyone about the special sale. It's a secret.'

'He's really good,' I said, 'at keeping secrets.'

Maybe she didn't hear me.

On the way home, we stopped back at the Terminal Diner. Maybe I'd spot a guy waiting, hoping against hope that his lost defective son would show up on the next bus from New York after all. The place smelled of leftovers being transformed into chilli. June, the afternoon-shift waitress, was turning half-empty bottles of ketchup into full new bottles with a balancing act straight out of a bankrupt circus. We'd gone on a couple of dates, back in high school and about a hundred pounds ago.

'Hey Juno...'

'Don't call me that.'

I was kinda touched. She still recognised my voice. 'Hey Juno, we heard there's a position available beyond yon swinging porthole door.'

She looked up, then. 'Sorry... Hey well now that you mention it... he's absolutely perfect.' Hire-the-handicapped incentives and tax easements flipped and clattered behind her eyes. She grabbed Adam's pudgy, limp but extremely dry hand. 'C'mon honey, let's go meet your new boss. Joe'll teach you what to do and maybe you can even start right away. There was an extra-large lunch crowd today.'

'Wait a minute...' My dream gig went poof in a bubble of divine justice. June the waitress wanted to do a civic good deed even more than she wanted to gloat on a college boy busted down to dishwasher in a greasy diner. So I kept my trap shut.

Maybe they needed someone at the Public Library. Figured I'd better make inquiries without Adam.

He eventually emerged from the kitchen, dressed for life's reality party in a heavy-duty black rubber apron and gloves and a paper hat on his head.

'Come pick him up around eleven,' June said. 'Dinner shift's usually done by then.'

The near-futurescope showed me and Mert staring at each other across a yellow-and-pink birthday cake while an excess pound of excellent ground meat endured Alaskan temperatures in the lime-green fridge Mert bought in nineteen fifty-five.

No need to ask Adam if washing dishes was what he really wanted to do. He could get diner-weight dishes and coffee cups as clean as anyone. And maybe I could step in for him, once I solved the mystery of his mother. In the meantime, Adam would learn the route between Mert's place and the diner, and get used having his own set of keys. 'Way to go, Adam. Mert and I are real proud of you. And I'm sure June and Joe will give you dinner here, so we can have our birthday party tomorrow night, instead.'

'Oh yeah... I forgot,' Adam said, and smacked his forehead a bit too hard. 'Maybe we could...'

'Never mind, Ad. Remember, today's the day we get to do whatever we want.'

'Oh, yeah. What do *you* want to do?'

Lay a deep alcoholic base at the Flame Bar & Grill's happy hour? Pick up a Secretary College sophomore? Buy an axe at the hardware store and butcher Mert the way I wanted to back in tenth grade, just for the hell of it? 'I want to watch you scrub your first professional frying pan, Adam. Too bad I don't have a camera. Got a camera, Juno?'

'Oh sure. I keep one handy to snap all the famous people who constantly stop by.'

Framed autographed picture of Senator Joe Biden nailed up behind the cash register, next to a way-below-felony-grade counterfeit three-dollar bill and a Pennsylvania road map. They hadn't yet put up the aqua-and-melon choking prevention signs that were all the mandated rage in New York.

Andy was a demon with a Brillo pad. Under his ministrations, greased-over porcelain, glass and aluminium soon sparkled. He gleamed, a rainbow soapbubble-cluster in his hair.

The Public Library wasn't on the way home, but I made the detour. Never exactly haunted the place, back in the days when it might've done me some good. Thought I knew just about everything I needed to know, then.

Must've looked like yet another tramp chugging in, minus the usual bizarre burdens stuffed into shopping bags.

When I finished filling out the job application form, the assistant librarian, a girl I knew slightly in high school, definitely not the car date type, said don't hold your breath for this plum. The library drew volunteer slave labour galore, in the form of bent hags familiar with the alphabet if not the Dewey decimal system, able to give directions, if asked politely and in a loud voice. Scranton municipal taxes didn't pay for a whole lot of Public Library, she said. Fewer patrons every year, fewer donations. Then she asked about life in the big city during the crazy, rage-y years. She asked if I'd ever gone to Studio 54, so I made up stories about wild nights, fabulous parties. Maybe she would've said yes to a date. Maybe even a car date, if she had a car.

The library was preserved, practically embalmed. Familiar formaldehyde smell in the reading room. I went to the main desk, filled out request forms for some medical books. When I scribbled Museum of Modern Art in the Professional Affiliation box, the librarian treated me as though I were a visiting dignitary from Culturania, a planet barely visible from Earth with naked eyes.

The afternoon stretched, while the winter waited courteously outside. It was warm in the library, but even the bums seemed to have deserted Scranton.

The nineteenth century English doctor who lent his name to what was wrong with Adam hara-kiri'd a potentially brilliant career when he chose to specialise in imbeciles and idiocy. He was convinced the appearance of external racial characteristics in certain individuals across the human spectrum was proof of universal brotherhood, that humankind's alleged races were one.

After I handed back the medical books I'd been studying, I took a trip through the Help Wanted sections in area newspapers.

Machine shop was my best subject in high school. The other guys thought the fix was in, since my pop was a mechanic. Teachers' pets had a way of getting beaten up, so I dropped the subject, in favour of English lit. Maybe that was the first step in the wrong direction. But I remembered some basics, like how the piston fits in the cylinder and gets pushed violently down when the gas spurts and explodes.

The rest, I could figure out.

The man who ran the garage and gas station just outside Tunkhannock said he'd take me on for a three-month trial at minimum wage. He also said I could use the courtesy beater car until a customer needed it. And he'd better not catch me filling the tank on the sly. That was the last guy's racket, and he had to leave town in a hurry.

Petty gas thief probably rode out on the bus I rode in on.

The lady at the uniform store was someone else I went to high school with. Major same-high-school-osis epidemic, blazing through Scranton. Bette Leffmeier, former prime car-date sweater-meat who'd stuck to her life's mission of filling out sweaters, gave me an embroidered name patch for free, offered to sew it on my new blue jumpsuit. Bette knew Mert wasn't up to threading needles any more, not that she'd ever done much sewing or embroidering.

My pop didn't have to wear a nameplate on his coveralls, because the customers knew who he was. He pretty much gave up on coveralls when he became the boss of his place, but his place was gone. Couldn't even give him the satisfaction of bestowing a tail-between-legs mercy hire. He'd dropped out of high school, volunteered to fight the Axis and wound up in a New Orleans supply depot instead. His mission was to prepare invasion craft and armoured half-tracks for delivery to where the action was. No shortage of action in New Orleans though, according to him. He learned plenty ropes. Crazy stories I wasn't supposed to breathe a word about to Mert or people like her friend Teeter who need to blab as much as breathe. But I couldn't remember the name of the garage where he started out. He told me, though. Must've told me a hundred times.

Popular culture has a huge impact on our daily lives, but it's notoriously difficult to write about. Tim Dunbar's story of music and identity shows us how it's done, and took second place in the Fiction Desk Newcomer Prize.

A Series of Circles

Tim Dunbar

'You look just like David Bowie, only more handsome.'

I was at the Cucumber Club for the Shrimp Bastards / Lugubrious Intent split bill, in line for a beer, when I simultaneously heard these words and felt a woman's firm yet supple left breast press against my right arm. Make no mistake: a man knows a breast when he feels one. Could be a bulletproof vest and ten parkas between a breast and a man and still he'll know one touched him. I turned my head to the right and beheld the owner of that breast, and another one just like it, sliding her left hand up my right arm, resting it on my shoulder, and beaming an I've-got-your number smile. She wore a tight black v-neck, cut-off jean shorts and flip-flops. Brown hair, brown eyes. Slightly tan and oh-so-lean. She had to be a good ten years younger than me. Which meant early twenties. Good god.

'Oh yeah?'

'Have you ever seen *Labyrinth*?'

I hadn't seen it. I wanted to see it so badly.

'No, I haven't. I really mean to, uh, you know, it's on my list. Would you believe someone once told me I should be *Labyrinth* David Bowie for Halloween?' Champion comment there, lad. 'Has he been in any other movies?'

Her hand still on my shoulder. The breast pressed in again.

'Oh God, where you have been? So many movies: *Last Temptation of Christ*, *Twin Peaks*, *Basquiat*. But my favourite is this uber strange one called *The Man Who Fell To Earth*. It's totally crazy.' The direct boldness of her gaze teetered me.

'I really have got to check that out.' Sincerely, obviously. 'So you like his acting and his music? I'm a huge fan of his musical output. What a body of work, right?'

Musical output? Body of work? Who's doing the talking here? I didn't own a single David Bowie album. I knew the guitar parts to 'Space Oddity' and 'Suffragette City' from my college cover band, Plato and the Cavemen. I fingered my wedding band. Twisted it round. My wife had just left town, took our kids to visit her father in Sioux City for a week.

'Yeah, so... irresistible.' My hair is what she was playing with at that exact moment.

Out of the corner of her eye she examined my Ludwig Wittgenstein 'Silence' T-shirt. 'Is that Johnny Cash?'

'No, it's actually...'

Suddenly she wheeled around and laced her fingers behind my neck. Full frontal contact now. She pressed into me.

'My name is Lady Stardust and I'm buying your beer, David Bowie. What're you drinking tonight?'

I swallowed hard. 'Uh, IPA?'

And with that she leaned in and planted a wet, three-second, slight-trace-of-tongue kiss directly on my lips.

Our turn in line. Our? She turned and ordered two PBRs. I hate PBR, everything about it. At that moment two dudes (Jeff Spicoli dudely dudes) inopportunely joined her at the bar. Each looked higher than the Space Needle.

'And some shots of Maker's Mark for my roommates! And for you too!' Not me too. The goddam bartender too. He obsequiously poured, downed, went back to business. Lady Stardust handed me my beer without a word and engaged Space Needle dudes in meaningless banter.

I lingered. Awkwardly in retrospect. Five seconds. Ten seconds. Thirty seconds. Nothing. She disappeared up the stairs to the balcony with Needle Dee and Needle Dum. If I followed it would be creepy and I knew it. Still I lingered. I was lost, out of my league. And I hate watching shows from the balcony.

I lingered too long. When I re-entered the main area of the club it was jam packed and my prime spot near the front, up against the first tier railing, was gone. Long gone. Got stuck in the rear behind a college kid just maddeningly slightly taller than me, and next to a chick who smelled of motor oil. Kid kept swaying in a herky jerky motion that sent his unkempt mop into my field of vision every few seconds. The Shrimp Bastards kicked ass, kind of an atonal take on the Ramones: math rock without losing the plot, if you feel me, practically coming apart at the seams, teetering on the edge the way good rock and roll should, complete with each musician first-named Shrimpy. But I was not enjoying myself. Why was I such a bonehead? I'd traded my good spot for a temporary chubb, a cheap kiss, and a beer I didn't even like.

In between sets I angled for a better view but there was none to be found. Sold out show, you know. My one stroke of luck came when Unkempt Mop vomited and subsequently fell over the third tier railing; not far, thankfully for all involved. I moved into his spot for Lugubrious Intent. They showed no mercy and surprised me with a slowed down, billowing version of 'Suffragette City'. My idea of a good cover is not a note-for-note copy of the original: no, a band needs to bring its own special chemistry, in pitched battle with that which makes the original continuously magical. Lugubrious Intent did just that. The singer, Conor O'Conor, made Bowie's fierce lyrics sound less like a minor threat and more like a cry for help. Pretty cool, but despite my unhindered view I still wasn't close enough to dance.

Post-show found me meandering back towards the bar, towards the merch table, trying to be cool. Chatted with the guitar player from Lugubrious Intent. Bought a T-shirt. I didn't see Lady Stardust anywhere so I exited the club. Couldn't quite bring myself to leave. I knew she was probably drunk off her ass but, but, but I don't know. Bummed a cigarette so I had an excuse to stand around and watch (nonchalantly, right?) for her to emerge. One drag. Two drags. Fourteen drags and no more cigarettes. She did not appear.

Feeling like an ass, I hurried back to my car, drove home, and masturbated vigorously (not in the car, but almost) to the memory of those breasts, those fingers, that kiss. It felt good but it didn't satisfy.

Confused and angry at myself, I drank half a fifth of gin, Navy Strength, and passed out. On a piece of furniture. I think.

Awoke the next morning on the floor with my head pressed hard into some patterned pillow, pounding with remorse. But for why? For drinking gin straight because who drinks gin straight, for the kiss, for the fleeting thrilling thought of infidelity. Even so, my first thought was of her. Stumbled into the kitchen, pissed in the sink, and reheated some day-old coffee on the stove while boiling water for a fresh French press. Added a shot of bourbon to ease the headache. Flipped open my laptop, punched in *craigslist.com*, and hurriedly clicked on missed encounters. As if.

'You said I looked like David Bowie only more handsome. At the Cucumber Club. Shrimp Bastards / Lugubrious Intent show 6/27/14. You made an impression on me. I want to know you.'

Confirm post. Hesitate. Oh God, what is wrong with me? What the hell am I doing? I want to know you? Jesus Christ. I want to know you. I want... what do I want to know?

Hold the phone. I immediately realised what I wanted to know. Goddam yes! The feeling in my brain was like when you flip on a light switch and the bulb pops unexpectedly.

Am I really more handsome than David Bowie?

I stood up, went into the bathroom, and peered into the mirror. Kettle whistled. Grabbed a comb and some hair gel and swirled my blond locks while violently waving a hairdryer. A caricature of an idea of Bowie. Like hell I'm handsome, let alone more handsome. I'm late-thirties ordinary and starting to show it.

Rushed back to the laptop and searched for *Labyrinth* David Bowie. Selected images. Holy eighties Batman! I look nothing like that David Bowie. Crazy bitch! Searched only David Bowie. Images. A bewildering assortment assailed me. Hair. Makeup. Body structure. Shape shifting. Tectonic plates scraped past each other in my soul. Just who is this David Bowie that I am supposedly more handsome than? Which one? Why couldn't she have said Springsteen? I know a hell of a lot about Springsteen and he's one handsome sonofabitch. Goddam David Bowie.

In that numinous moment I stopped caring about Lady Stardust and became obsessed with David Bowie. Then I put the coffee on.

I studied pictures half the morning, strangely fascinated. Bowie has more versions of himself than Bob Dylan. Was I Ziggy Stardust? Not cool enough. *Diamond Dogs?* Not weird enough. *Aladdin Sane?* A bit. *Hunky Dory?* Oh mother. *Heroes?* Meaning obscured. *The Buddha of Suburbia?* I wish. *Heathen?* Ultimate suave. What next? I had the day off. Shit, it's Saturday. Obviously I had the day off. Went to the main public library and looked for books about David Bowie. *Bowie: Album by Album. David Bowie: Starman. David Bowie: The Biography. The Complete David Bowie* — holy shit that's quite a word count. Checked them the fuck out. Wasted no daylight getting to my favourite record store and bought a truckload of Bowie. Cleaned them out completely. Asked the clerk who Bowie had collaborated with, recorded with, produced, did they have bootlegs, posters, T-shirts, bobbleheads, snow globes, Kewpie dolls, guitar picks, anything David Bowie. Vinyl, CD, old cassettes, duplicates. It didn't matter — I had to have it. The kid seemed slightly unnerved. I don't know why.

My wife called as I drove home.

'Hi, honey, what're you up to?'

'Nothing much, just out and about. How was your flight? Kids do okay?'

'Yeah, they were easy. The plane had movies so they watched some kids' movie I've never heard of. I just read. Pretty easy. Then they fell asleep in the car on the way to the house.'

'How's your dad?'

'Nothing changes with him. You owe me for giving you a week to yourself. How was the show?'

'Show was good, really good, but I got stuck in a shitty spot. Lugubrious Intent did a killer cover of "Suffragette City".'

'Suffragette City?'

'Yeah, you know. That David Bowie song.'

'No.'

Back at the house that afternoon I threw *Ziggy Stardust* on the turntable, powered on my work laptop, and opened Photoshop. Copied several pictures of different era David Bowies, mostly album covers, along with several pictures of myself, and imported them all. Pasted my face onto different era Bowie faces and vice versa. To see which one I looked more handsome than, to see which one I had to top. Let's see. Vacation-in-the-mountains me on *Pin Ups*. *Space Oddity* Bowie on finishing-a-marathon me. Long-haired-college me on *Hunky Dory* Bowie. *Black Tie White Noise* Bowie on at-a-charity-fundraiser me. Several others I won't mention. They all looked asinine. With good reason though: his were painstakingly set up artistic shots; mine just random photos. I needed to get myself into the mood of the album cover I wanted to match, or as close as I could. *Scary Monsters* took a spin on the turntable. I sheepishly snuck into my own master bathroom and dug through what makeup my wife had left behind. Never been this way before. Pretty, so pretty. I set up my camera and timer and took scores of self-shots. Sucked my cheeks in, struck a pose. Got quite into it, actually. That's more like it. Tease the hair, fuck with it, make it your bitch. Change the clothes, put on a dress, take off your top. And above all powder powder powder. Float like a butterfly.

I spent four hours hosting and documenting my own fashion show. That's cool. I'm all alone: I should get to do what I want, not worry about wasting time, all that utilitarian concern that comes with a family. Imported the pictures with anxious anticipation. Pasted those in.

Float like a butterfly. *Let's Dance.*

That's it! *Let's Dance.* I am more handsome than *Let's Dance* era David Bowie. Not bad, not bad at all. Discovering this brought me great elation. But God what a quiff! Or is that a perm? It's a bit late in the day for a hair appointment.

Sunday. I went to church. Felt like I was in on a secret that I couldn't tell anyone, but not about David Bowie, not about the kiss, not about the breasts. I didn't know what. I was one of countless husbands, polite yet uninvolved, who went through the worship workout because it was important to his wife. Just there, existing, enduring. Zero-gravity smile and a collared shirt.

The priest droned on. Then something he said snapped me out of my reverie and inscribed itself on my mind like chalk on a virgin chalkboard. Something about our personalities morphing and spiralling around a constant centre. That blew my mind, and I wasn't accustomed to having my mind blown whilst sitting in a pew. Fucking Jesuits. Always walking on the goddam moon.

Monday. I hauled the albums to work. Listened to them all day. I had a corner office on the eleventh floor of a hip advertising firm where I laboured as chief design editor. I made excuses (conference call, urgent deadline, software glitch) to miss meetings so I wouldn't forsake the Bowie. Decided to go chronologically, instil some discipline in this endeavour, and had to default to a few less-than-legal sources to fill in the gaps from my record store purchases. It was a bit painful, I hate to say, because I couldn't connect with much before *Hunky Dory* even though I heard the influence of *The Man Who Sold the World* in many of the bands I listened to as a teenager. Got up to *Young Americans* before the whistle blew. Picked up an uncharacteristic greasy burger and fries and upon arriving home stuck my greasy little fingers into *David Bowie: Album by Album.*

Yeaaaaaaaaah, I honed in on the early seventies stuff. Who doesn't, initially? How could you not? 'Life on Mars?' rang out from the speakers like a call to prayer. What is the space fascination? 'Space Oddity' (come on, it is pretty much seventies) hit the shelves within months of the moon landing and had to be studio finished somewhere around the same time and conceived even earlier. In the sixties and seventies the space race was still fast and close enough to dominate the imagination of populace and presidents alike, unlike now where it dominates the imagination of Richard Branson and the moneyed elite. Back then everything was rocket boosters, jet fuel and thrust, moonwalks and space helmets. Titan rockets climaxing left and right. Space was the final frontier but now, as with poetry, we don't give a fuck. For exactly the same reasons. The transcendent, while fading, still cast enough starlight to capture our imagination. Today everything is immanent, urgent, cross-pressured. But the rub is that we were grinning apeshit when space was the final frontier, and now that we know it isn't, we've lost interest. Too far to care, I guess. Fifty, forty years ago we could still lose ourselves in utopian daydreams while suppressing the correlative nightmares. Today ten per cent of the daydreams and one-hundred-and-ten per cent of the nightmares have come true and we don't want to close our eyes anymore unless under the influence of heavy narcotics. But David Bowie never suffered our common disenchantment, not as far as I could tell. Album by album, he never abandoned space.

Tuesday. Called in sick. Spent aeons on the internet, in the books, with seventies Bowie for my soundtrack. Investigated arcane aspects of glam rock sexuality. Just for kicks took out a pair of stockings from my wife's drawer and slashed a few holes in them, put them on with a baggy tank top and a scarf. Best I could do so fuck off. My cat sat on a chair and gave me a look that said

'You ridiculous human.' I felt a strange shame. Because of the cat. I hadn't realised Bowie went through a bisexual period, or so they say. I'd never given my sexual preferences a second thought. How media and culture shaped were they? Nature nurture and all that shit. What if a pale, slender, androgynous young white man had brushed up against me and complimented my visage? What if it had been a forty-something black woman? A man just like me? Your grandmother. Thoughts like these put me out to sea in a land where I have no bearing. But they're not useful. Lady Stardust was just my type and she turned me on alright. What are her preferences? To flirt with #juststartingtoage men, turn them on to David Bowie, and then tag-team kite-high drunk boy roommates.

Wednesday night. Tonight's the night. Eighties night. It had been eighties day with Bowie: *Scary Monsters* through *Tin Machine* (who kicked ass, I must say). I decided to get high and watch *Labyrinth*. Why? I couldn't say, but it seemed meet and right so to do. If the spandex fits, ya know? So do I ask my neighbours who smoke for a little help or go to a dispensary – shit is legal where I live. But if I buy my name is in the registry, right? I assume they (they?) have a registry (registry?) for these things (these things?).

At the dispensary, Gooseberry Grass, I felt like a buffoon. Same as every other late thirty-something who hasn't smoked since college and doesn't want a harsh mellow, just a cool buzz. But it was just me projecting. The people working there were quite welcoming. No registry, just ID please. Sat in the waiting room until my name was called to the backroom where an overeager young man benignly assaulted me with sativa and indica and did I know that justification for pot is in the Bible, and boy was I exceedingly glad that the place sold five dollar pre-rolls. When I returned home a new problem faced me: where to smoke it?

Backyard would spread the obvious smell. Inside is definitely off limits. Walk to a nearby park, smoke, then walk back? Drive to that parking lot by the elementary school? What if I can't find my way home? What if the effects wear off before I get into the movie? In the end I...

...risked the basement. It was soooooooo worth it.

Turns out my tolerance for marijuana is halfway decent and two joints in I had one hell of a time entering the *Labyrinth*. In chemically aided HD. The plot is thinner than rolling paper but I had to hand it to the puppet people because for the eighties that was a magnificent job. And I take back the crazy bitch comment: I could see how Lady Stardust might find *Labyrinth* Bowie and his tight pants package attractive. The excitement of David Bowie, indeed!

Thursday. Stepped onto my back porch head-on into the lower corner of a huge spiderweb in which a massive spider sat poised to catch prey, to keep prey out of my home. When had it built this? Yeah, I get it, Spiders from Mars playing tricks on my brains. Walked back inside, brushed spider's thread out of my *Let's Dance* quiff, and examined my stack of Bowie albums. Nothing beckoned. Grabbed the laptop and inquired 'David Bowie concert T-shirt?' Found a sleeveless T-shirt on eBay from his Serious Moonlight tour, nineteen eighty-three. Perfect *Let's Dance* hair in fourfold glory. Sixty dollars. Overnight shipping hell yes.

Restless and dissatisfied I about-faced to the stack of albums. Put on *Earthling* but it didn't move me. Gooseberry had a two-for-one going last night so I fired up pudgy joint number three while cracking open a, uh, PBR. Not gonna waste good beer on weedtongue so forgive the hypocrisy. Replaced *Earthling* with *Heathen* and as 'Slip Away' slow burned I realised I'm six days in. My mind wondered what was sustaining this impulsive and nevralgic excursion into Bowieland? As if the fantastic music, the fascinating fashion, the daring artistic exploration, the sheer muse of it all weren't enough. These were more than compelling but if a man in a trench coat stopped me on the street and asked me to explain the past six days of my life what rational answer would I proffer? There had to be some soul connection, didn't there? Was this an identity crisis for which I had Lady Stardust to thank? No, no, no. As I philosophised the THC did its work and I slipped into a trance. Astral visions spun before me, crab nebula supernova, black holes, shattered remnants of massive stars, Messier 82, M83, galactic wreckage, spirals of cosmic dust, galaxies and celestial wonders. I travelled faster than the speed of light yet experienced utter stillness, and imagined I heard David Bowie's baritone intoning the words that gave purpose to my search: 'Who do you say that I am?'

I woke up in sheets of sweat, in a panic. I'm a fraud. I can't compete. I knew I couldn't stand a chance against the diehard fans. If you discovered Bowie as a teenager in the seventies he changed the whole world, but me, he'd only changed my world. You can't ever worship like you did at sixteen, in your teenage years, when you gathered sacred things into your heart. I was lucky enough that Dylan found me in my teens, when he could still get a foothold, but every classic artist I've put off until my older days hasn't made the same dent. So why did David Bowie grip my heart? Who would I say that he is? There are no shortcuts to the answer.

Friday. One week since my last concert and I learned to my devastation that I am too late. I will never see David Bowie live in concert. Not at the Cucumber Club. Not at Madison Square Garden. Not anywhere at all. Found out his last public performance was in two thousand and six. And not even a proper David Bowie concert at that. He has ascended, never to grace the earth again, and sits at his own right hand. In this way he has become utterly transcendent, an interfering agent who periodically drops miracles of recorded sound from outside the space/time continuum. Take that you freaky Jesuits. He has achieved... uh, achieved... um...

My new ringtone (China Girl) snapped me out of it.

It was a number I didn't recognise. Had I accidentally posted the Craig's List missed connections ad? Oh no.

'This is Chris at Gooseberry Grass. You left your driver's licence here. Been trying to reach you for two days.'

'My driver's licence. Right.'

Saturday. I returned to the Cucumber Club in full *Let's Dance* regalia to see a Talking Heads cover band. A bunch of kids stared hard at me. But they didn't know. They hadn't entered the world of David Bowie. As the David Byrne lookalike sang, I became overwhelmed by the universe I had entered. What was that about a morphing and spiralling personality with a constant centre? David Bowie is a world, no, worlds unto himself, and I found myself being led further and further down the rabbit hole. History legend mythology music stage film books websites side projects lovers wives opinions speculations. It had taken me eighteen years to realise I'd never understand Dylan and that realisation was the clue to grabbing a fraction of an understanding, knowing that I'd touched something mysterious. In its turn, that touch, that knowledge of unknowing, was enough to sustain the search. Not surprising, therefore, that one week into Bowie the prospect of reaching that same virgin point neutralised my ambition and caused my brain pain thinking about the investment. But I couldn't turn my back, forget how far I'd come in one week, pretend I had other, better things to do. As for answering the question, the songs would serve as my lexicon, my prayer book.

My faith is in the songs. But this generation doesn't know the names of songs anymore, just track numbers, just how to find one in a digital library. But with David Bowie we know the names of the songs. How could we not know?

Sunday. Returned to church. I felt blessedly in touch with my humanity, and when the woman next to me earnestly asked about my week I enthusiastically told the truth, that I had a great week, and you? But to my distress she didn't want to hear about my great week. She wanted self-authenticity which in her mind was only pain and struggle, terrible lives lived outside these holy halls, things kept hidden revealed, my deepest self, my longings, my fears, my unhoped hopes. Why can't joy be authentic? And if not then I didn't know why I was at church.

'Hi honey. Uh, honey? I can't hear you.'
    'Sorry.' I turned down 'It's No Game (Part I)', a totally normal song for me to listen to at an extremely loud volume while making a tuna fish sandwich.
    'So it looks like our flight is on time. Can't wait to see you!'
    'Cool cool. Can't wait to see you too! I'll pick you up at the curb. Text me when you land.'
    Shit! The basement. It smelled like the Bog of Eternal Stench. I rushed down, opened every window, turned on every fan, then raced to Nick's Knacks, bought fifteen scented candles, and lit the place up.
    Five hours later...
    'You, uh, you look different.' I wore the Serious Moonlight tour shirt and (did I forget to mention) had bleached my hair. Nothing major.
    My kids looked for their father. But only for one fraction of a second. Their 'Daddy!' did me in.

I jumped forward and embraced them with abandon, as only a man who has had a life changing experience can, as only a man who has been deprived of his family for a week can. We picked up a pizza on the way home and watched *Labyrinth*, crammed on our tiny couch, laughing and crying.

Turned out my wife actually liked the new hairstyle. And when we made love that night I looked straight into her eyes and held them for longer than ever before.

Two months later, I stepped onto the elevator, americano in hand, clear head on my shoulders. My affair with Bowie had settled into an ember glow and I was content, content in every way, content to let Bowie's universe stretch out before me, vast and believable, while I explored it grain by grain of sand.

Lady Stardust stepped on at the fifth floor. Wonder of wonders. Her fingers laced around her cell phone, earbuds mosquito buzzing, her youth and vitality on full display. Only one fraction of a second did her mascara-lacquered eyes flit upwards before returning to the immanent, reassuring glow of the tiny screen.

I didn't say a word.

Better known for his comic writing, Adam Blampied here takes a serious and unnerving look at personal and social conflict.

The Cobble Boys

Adam Blampied

If you hear the Cobble Boys come running down your street,
If you hear the clatter noise of unseen ghostly feet,
And if they catch you on the road, not safe behind a door,
Then you'll run with the Cobble Boys, and run for evermore.

— Anon

The daylight is blazing itself out, leaving low sunlight, warm autumn browns in the trees. I drape the dishcloth over the back of my hand, fixing it tight around my knuckles with tape.

Outside the air is cool, a soft wind coming in with the night. I can still hear the children playing on the street, the snapping of their boot heels on the pavement. I can hear Sean out amongst them, yapping like a dog.

The backyard is filled with sheets, hung up and bulging in the breeze. I pass through the washing, through the shifting walls to the apple tree. The leaves are a bright burning orange, the apples blood-red spots peeking through. It's getting colder.

I run my fingertips over the bark. I flex my hand, making sure the cloth is tight around it, then I punch my fist hard against the wood. The cloth cushions my fingers a little, but still a jolt of pain crackles under my knuckles, up my arm.

From the street I hear mothers calling in their children. The panic notes in their voices. I hear Ma calling for Sean. I hear Mrs Kinnock banging a dustbin lid and calling for her own, for Jacob. She's shrieking for him. The sun is teetering on the horizon. I punch the tree again. The banging of the dustbin lid. The frightened shouts for Jacob. I punch again.

When I turn around, Sean is standing there, brown hair combed over the wreck of his face: his puffed up cheek, his swollen eye, the scratch marks where they forced his face to the stones, rubbed him against the gravel. He looks up at me and whispers, 'Dinner please Mary.'

We're not a family that's really involved, never have been, not even when Dad was alive. Because of that, the Clearys have been called cowards, unionists, protestants. Ma's been attacked in the market, mothers jumping on her and pulling at her hair. But it's been quiet enough now. We're just living in the wrong part of the city.

The Brits can't get their trucks into Free Derry. The barricades have stood, and we're living behind them. Bogside is going to be its own country, the boys are saying.

Ma doesn't look up at me when I come into the kitchen; instead she's lost over her glass. I untape my hand and set the table with Sean. He does the placemats and I do the cutlery.

Halfway through, there's a loud bang from a few streets over, Sackville Street or thereabouts. Inside the house though, dinner's quiet. It has been for years.

Once everything's settled up and put away, the darkness has set in and the street lamps are on. I peer out through the curtain. The street's deserted, not a soul from Waterloo Road to Chamberlain. A few years ago the kids would all still be out, you couldn't drag them in. You'd see mothers out in squads, with wooden spoons primed for bare legs: a militia in nighties collecting up wayward brats. But now they're all locked up tight, leaving only the mournful street lamps and the stillness.

'The Cobble Boys,' that's what I tell Sean, whenever he's inching near the door, itching for a run around. He's there tonight. He wants out, to turn the cold night air hot in his lungs. I take him upstairs to tell him the story.

I get him ready for bed. The bruise still takes up most of his right shoulder. It looks like a large puddle of dirt and oil on his pale skin. He washes his face, but I say he can leave his teeth tonight: it hurts too much to brush. He lies down and I put the blankets on him.

'The Cobble Boys,' I say, 'well it's not that I believe it myself, but you do hear these whisperings. These whisperings...' I turn off his bedside lamp, 'in the shadows...'

He's mine by that point, his little mouth hanging open and daft.

'This was years and years and years ago, back when it was horse and carts everywhere, before our grandfathers' time. They say they used to be a gang – nothing like today though, not that kind. They were a friend gang, you know. Pals. Normal kids.'

He nods.

'They stuck pins in their shoes,' I say. 'The metal ones, flat, into their heels. That was their little thing. They'd stud themselves up and off they'd run through the streets at night. Every night they'd be out pounding the cobbles, waking the neighbours. This long clattering noise up and down the street. The metal hitting the cobbles, clatter, clatter. That's why they say — do you remember what they say?'

He pauses. He's got his blankets up to his nose by this point. He speaks, softly. No more than a whisper in the darkness.

'"If you hear the Cobble Boys come running down your street. If you hear the clatter noise of unseen ghostly feet..." What do they look like now? Like ghosts?'

'Well you're not supposed to know, are you? You're supposed to get inside, behind the door. Back then, though, they were just kids, just normal boys. Story has it they were out one night. Out on the street, they were running, like every night. One of the little boys runs out across the road. He doesn't see the cart until it's on top of him. He's pulled under the horse, under the cart. Stone dead in seconds. The rest of the boys, they can't take it, they lose their minds.'

Sean shivers.

'It drives them insane, losing one of their own. They break the horse's legs, go for its eyes, slash — no, *pull* — its belly open. The two fellas in the cab, they get out and they run. They run and run as fast as they can, but all they can hear behind them, behind them all the way home, is the clattering of metal on the cobbles.'

'Then what happens?' Sean whispers.

'Nothing that night, but every night after that, when the sun went down and the roads were quiet, the two men, from behind their door, out on the street, what did you think they could hear?'

'The clatter noise...'

'One night not long after, one of the men went out walking, just for a pint a few streets over, and he didn't come home. Not that night, or any night. He was never seen again. No trace of his body, ever. But do you know what people heard that night, out in the street?'

'The clatter noise of unseen ghostly feet...'

'The other fella moved away, they said. Moved down to Cork, eventually over to London. Set up a glove-making company, lived a few years. Then he went out one night and he didn't come home. The police never found him, but his housekeeper, what did she say she heard that night, up and down the street outside? "The clatter noise of unseen ghostly feet."'

Sean gulps with nerves, then tries to smile it off, showing his cracked teeth.

'Sammy Keegan says she hears running at night. Near the flats.'

'Aye,' I say. 'You hear tales from all over, for years and years. And that's why we never go out after dark, isn't it? That's why we lock the doors. That's why we behave. "And if they catch you on the road, not safe behind a door..."'

'Then you'll run with the Cobble Boys, and run for evermore.'

I brush his hair back one more time, exposing the marks that cover most of his forehead, his temple, his cheek. They held his face down.

'And you're sure it was the McKaids?' I ask.

He doesn't say anything, just looks at me.

'You have to be sure,' I say.

He nods.

'Okay,' I say, then kiss him lightly on the forehead, where the skin is still pale and unbroken.

I head downstairs and into the kitchen. I take the dishcloths from the sideboard and begin taping my knuckles again. As I finish one and move on to the other I notice that Ma has joined me. She doesn't say anything, but sits at the table, pouring herself something from one of the green bottles I sometimes find hidden in the cupboards, between the sofa cushions, under her bed. She takes her drink in her thin hands and looks at me. I can't read anything from her face, so I get on with taping my other hand. When I take the one spotted with strawberries she mutters:

'You could have the courtesy to not use me best fucking towel.'

I keep taping.

'I'll wash it.'

She finishes her drink and reaches for the bottle.

'As long I don't have to pick it off you. When they found your father they'd taken his wallet, his watch, his handkerchief.'

'I said I'll fucking wash it.'

'I'll peel it off you, Mary, and that'll be that, I suppose.'

I look at her. She's the youngest old woman I've ever seen, or the other way round. In the last few years she's shrunk, folded into herself, let her own shoulders force her down into a rough bargain copy of the woman she once was.

'What would you like me to do?' I ask. 'Tell them that coming after you, me, Sean, that's going – we're just gonna take it? Might as well give them the key to the fucking door.'

'You sound like the young fellas, the students. Everything got to have an answer.'

I finish my fists. I grab my coat from the hook and put it on, rolling the sleeves down to conceal the cloth around my hands.

'It's a fucking waste,' Ma says, blocking my path, 'your dad knew that. Let them give it back and give it back, aye, but not you, me, or Sean. Not my little boy!'

'And how did keeping out of it work for Dad?' I shout over her.

I expect her to hit me but she doesn't. She just walks away, taking the bottle with her. It bangs against the bannister as she climbs the stairs. She doesn't look around but walks to her bedroom and closes the door.

The house is still. I stand in the darkness, listening. There is nothing, no noise from the street. I'm caught in a moment, I can tell. The lads talk about it, you feel yourself caught in important times. Opportunities, they say, to do something. I feel that now, standing there in the hall, looking at the front door. The opportunity to do something un-ignorable. The opportunity not to, as well. The lads tend to forget that one, the choice to not do it. What that means, the difference between letting something go and casting it aside. I see that, all of the choices, right now.

And I step out onto the street.

The terraced houses are all dark. The sheer wall of identical doors and windows is quiet and disappears off into the shadows. There are a few muffled squares of light from curtained windows, but there is a deadness to the street. You feel it in the air. The wind has disappeared and there's a balmy heaviness. The air feels bloated, and sick. I feel like I'm waiting. Ill and waiting.

I set off towards Abbey Park. That's where they'll be.

I walk alone in the quiet, crossing Chamberlain Street with the twin cars, burned out and wheelless. They're brittle and thin. The kids have kicked a hole straight through the metal on one side. There's still that smell of burnt leather. The windows are shut and bolted all along here and Eden Street beyond.

Eden opens onto a courtyard and I see two of the DCDA, the Bogside defenders: one of the Walker boys and I don't know the other one. Both of them, barely older than me, twenty-something, making a big point of their pellet guns and knives, keeping them on display. They're just off the main road, crouching near the wire fence.

The one I don't know looks up at me as I pass, but they're not the trouble tonight. They're not even after protestants. They want police blood, since the gas.

I see a small supply of bottles at their feet, rags sticking out, and there's the sickly smell of petrol as I walk by.

It was on the corner there, down on Rossville that the police used the gas. I saw them staggering home to their mums and dads, red-eyed and spluttering. You can't feel it anymore, the air's lost its prickle, but the road's still littered with broken bricks and stones.

Rossville's empty at my end, but further up the road you can see the barricade, and a few fellas keeping watch. It's more of a heap than a wall. A barbed wire fence runs across the road, the gaps filled in with wooden planks, great hunks of plaster and stone, a few empty barrels. It's a jagged mess but it's kept out the trucks. Beyond the barricade is The Corner, as it's getting to be known. The corner of Rossville and Lecky, one of the walls of the buildings has been whitewashed, and you can see the words painted large and black:

YOU ARE NOW ENTERING FREE DERRY.

The boys declared themselves their own little kingdom, built with stones, planks and petrol.

Down Lecky Road is where they found my father, face down on the pavement, with a bullet in the back of his head. He wasn't a unionist or a nationalist or anything. He was just my dad, and he died for nothing.

I stay away from the barricade and cut down an alley. There's something about joining the IRA sprayed on the wall in white. I keep walking and the alley opens out into the parks. Here the terraces and flats are grouped in squares, a large courtyard surrounded by housing on four sides. I pass through Glenfada park, which is deserted, all the doors closed, the lights off. I move around the furthermost houses and turn the corner to see Abbey Park. At the centre of the courtyard are three trees and two street lamps. Under the nearest lamp are the McKaids, all five of them.

They've got about two faces and one haircut between them. They've taken Abbey Park for themselves and since they've been running errand duty for the defenders and, according to rumour, running door-to-door for some of the IRA, they've got a sense of importance about themselves, and ownership right along with it. They straighten up as they see me approach.

'Right,' I say, standing in front of the small clump of McKaid genes. 'One of you is getting the shit kicked out of ya. Which one?'

Michael, the eldest McKaid, is eating some sort of meat wrapped in greaseproof paper. When I finish speaking, he laughs and a small fleck of the stuff hits me on the cheek. The other boys follow suit, chuckling and nudging each other.

I wipe it away, then take off my coat, exposing my dishcloth-covered hands. This doesn't have the effect I'd hoped for; they fall apart laughing, clutching at each other.

'Listen, youse gormless fucks,' I shout, my face burning, 'the Clearys owe the McKaids a fucking kicking, now which will it be or will I fucking pick?'

'Ah come on now, Mary,' says Aidan, one of the younger ones. 'Judging from the size of him, I'd say you only owe us half a kicking.'

'That you volunteering, shitkicker?' I say, stepping forward. Aidan doesn't move.

'Thought the Clearys didn't fight,' says Michael through a mouthful of meat. 'Thought that was the point of you.'

'They killed your dad,' said Patrick, the littlest, about five years younger than me. 'Why you not out with a gun picking off Provos?'

'One of you just come on and take what's coming to you,' I say. I hope they can't see my right knee shaking. I can hardly hear myself, my blood's thundering in my ears.

'Piss off,' said Bill, the second eldest. 'Just a little reminder of where you were fucking born. If you're not gonna help, if you're not gonna pitch in, youse can fuck off or get worse.'

'He's a little fucking boy,' I shout, and I can see lights coming on in the houses of Abbey Park. Little squares of light dotting about in the corners of my vision. The boys see it too. 'You don't get to knock him around and walk away,' I say. 'Unless one of the bigger Clearys is too much for you?'

I say this loud enough for the houses to hear and that's when the boys decide to get serious.

'Ken, you've been fucking quiet,' says Michael. 'After all, you were the first one on the wee lad, eh?'

Ken steps forward. He looks embarrassed. He should. We were at fucking school together.

'Mickey, I can't, she's... you know,' he squirms.

'Fucking...' Michael whistles through his teeth in frustration. 'Just let her get a few fucking taps in then I dunno, pull her hair or something.'

Ken steps up to me. I'm giving away four inches to him easy. He gives a last look back to his brothers, then starts to speak.

'Listen, we were only —'

I bring my fist round to his jaw with all the power I can. My swing's too high and I get him on the cheekbone. Despite the coverings, my hand explodes with pain. Ken is knocked back into Aidan, but stays on his feet, his eyes wide with shock. The slicked curls of his hair have tumbled down to his eyes, and his face is flushed.

That was the best one I am going to get, and he didn't go over. I shake my fist out, try not to give on how much it hurts. I bring it round again, jump forward and plough my closed knuckles into his neck. He moves aside, and before I know where he's gone, a fist shoots from the darkness and catches me in the temple. The world goes white, there's a distant ring, and I fall aside, feeling the cold wet pavement on my skin, the tiny pieces of stone digging into my knees and the flat of my palms.

I look up and Michael is holding Aidan back. He delivers him a slap across the face.

'The fuck you're playing at,' he shouts. 'This is for fucking Ken.'

The brothers back away at that, a couple of paces, leave me and Ken alone under the bright pool of lamplight. He's breathing quickly. I can barely hear the sound of the other boys. They sound underwater, far away. We're both to our feet now, and I squeeze the dishcloths in my fists.

If you hear the Cobble Boys come running down your street...

He starts forward, ducks, and his shoulder catches me in the ribs, taking us both down onto our knees. He brings a fist into my ribs, but the pain feels numb and I wriggle free. I stagger to my feet and while he's still on one knee I kick him as hard as I can across the face. There's a loud snap as blood bursts from his nose.

He grabs my leg and lunges into me, forcing me over. My head cracks against the raised pavement and for a moment I don't know where I am, until he's on top of me. I hear distant cheers and claps as I clutch my head, pushing against him with one hand.

If you hear the clatter noise of unseen ghostly feet...

He grabs my head, grabs handfuls of hair, and swings me up. I don't know where I'm going, but my shoulder slams into something hard. I try to protect my face, reach around and feel the rough bark of a tree. I swing out again and my fist catches Ken in the teeth. I can feel the skin of my knuckles open. One of my fingers is bent the wrong way and the rest have a deep red gash running across the knuckles. The dishcloth is in rags and I can't make out the strawberries. It's all red.

And if they catch you on the road, not safe behind a door...

Ken doesn't grab me as much as throw his entire body at me. His weight slips but he lands across my legs and that brings me down. I put up my hands to stop him but they offer little resistance. He brings both his hands down on my shoulders, my collar, and tries to tear at my clothes.

Then you'll run with the Cobble Boys, and run for evermore.

The top of my head catches him on the chin, and blood immediately starts to flow onto my forehead. It feels like my head is on fire. I weakly get to my feet and wipe at the blood, smearing it away from my eyes. I see Ken, blurry, on his knees and I swing out with my foot. The point of my shoe catches him in the eye socket and he falls backwards, smacking his head against the tarmac.

My head is heavy and my balance keeps shifting, but the sensation of the cold night air comes back to me.

The boys are standing around Ken. He's not moving, and his right eye socket is a red mess, smashed and bloody. The boys stand around him, mouths open in shock, faces white, their eyes nothing but shadows from the lamplight overhead. He's not moving.

I start to walk away, I realise that I have to get away now, that it's over and that I have to go, I have to go now. I walk and it hurts, and I stagger but I keep moving. I hear a yell behind me and I lean forward and run. The motion hurts my head and my upper body feels so heavy.

I run through Glenfada park and onto Rossville. The world rushes past me, bouncing, still blurry, smeared a vague red. I keep running past the barricade and the boys with the petrol bombs and the knives and I keep running towards home. I can hear them though, behind me as I run, weak-legged and dripping blood.

I can hear them running, the clatter of their shoes. I can hear them getting closer.

Mark Newman's chilling look at our difficult relationship with the past won this year's Fiction Desk Newcomer Prize.

Before There Were Houses, This Was All Fields

Mark Newman

When I was at the end of my childhood, Susie Banshawe disappeared. For a while no one knew where she was, and that was the best of it. There was a sense of excitement, each of us hoping we would be the first to discover a clue, without really understanding what that meant.

We lived on a street called Crunching Croft and I bussed into school at Maple Bumpstead. It was like something out of a fairy tale, so we should have known. Give a housing estate fairy-tale names and something evil is bound to follow. But what would we have done with a happy ever after? To live happily ever after, to be happy day in, day out, and never to be plagued by nightmares when you slept. It would be as exhausting as being permanently unhappy. We are not meant to be one thing at all times.

It was a new estate, still being developed, buildings popping up all the time. We had a house you could run a circuit round inside. Is that unusual? I have not lived in a house like it since. From the hallway to the living room to the dining room to the kitchen and back into the hallway. You always had forward momentum. Even in the lounge if I wanted to get to the hall I would run through the dining room, into the kitchen and out into the hall again. I had my own one-way system in force.

All the houses were the same. Across from us an almighty pit had been dug, and around it more houses were being built. We ran around investigating, my best friend Jammy and I, standing at the edge of the pit and looking down. It was the first place anyone thought of looking of course, but they'd had teams down there, winching sniffer dogs down on pulleys, but with nothing to show for it. The shells of those half-built houses stood around, all bricks, breeze blocks, and concrete. They were like skulls, no windows in the eye sockets, and ladders propped where the stairs would be. Jammy and I clambered up those ladders and launched ourselves from upstairs windows onto mounds of sand below. There was no Health and Safety in those days; or if there was, nobody took much notice. When those houses were finished I stood in front of them, full of all the impressive knowledge you can feel when you're ten: I have seen your skull, I have seen you without your skin. I thought I knew those houses better than the people who lived in them. In some way they were all interlopers, spoiling my fun.

We had the run of the place, us kids. The best thing we did was follow the dustbin men. They let us sling the smaller things into the back of the truck. I loved the clang of the metal teeth, the way they devoured it all, whatever you fed them. I loved the smell of all that rotten food and the guys with their fluorescent clothes; their hands and faces covered in muck. They were feeling important too; the police had asked them to watch for anything being chucked that could give them a lead.

'You should come back to my place sometime,' one of them said. 'The things I find that people throw out, you wouldn't believe.'

'He's starting his own junk shop,' another one said. 'It's all there in his front room.'

They laughed a lot and slapped each other on the shoulders. When they did the same to Jammy and I, we thought we were real men; grown up and ready to face the world.

Policemen were appearing at odd moments all over the place; we got used to seeing them about. I ran into one down an alleyway. He asked if I'd seen anything suspicious in recent weeks. I told him all about a man I'd seen and gave a full description; I got really into it. He took out a pad and pen and jotted everything down I was saying. I believe he took it all quite seriously and when I'd finished he asked if I would go down to the station with him to give a statement. I said my mother would never allow it and ran off. In bed that night I lay awake worrying I had inadvertently described someone who lived in the neighbourhood. I imagined them being arrested and convicted on the strength of the testimony of a child with nothing better to do with his time than lie to policemen.

We ran about the place collaring small children, telling them if they didn't watch it they'd go the same way as Susie Banshawe;

then we worried one of them would cry and blab and we'd become the main suspects. Oh, why were we so cruel? We just did what older kids had done to us before, but that doesn't excuse it.

They found her of course, though it took three long weeks when all the adults were on edge and jumpy. She had been strangled and buried in a muddy plot of land at the edge of our estate. It was a foolish place to put her; the land was marked for building and she would have been discovered sooner or later but I suppose the killer was in a panic and could think of nothing better. They never caught him, never even got close it seems. Mysteries aren't meant to be left unsolved, are they?

I say 'they' found her, but it was me. I found her. Jammy and I were playing along the disused rail track that ran alongside the estate. All the kids went down there. There was a gap in one of the hedges you could squeeze through and run across the muddy plot of land to get home if you were due in for tea and needed to get back quick. I had new wellies on and half way across the muddy field my feet sank into the mud; one welly wedged solid. You'd think I was marooned in a cave with the tide coming in the fuss I made, screaming the whole place down. Jammy laughed his head off and shouted his goodbyes, not wanting to be late: his father could be a bit of a lout. I cried hot, childish tears which are the best kind to cry even in adult life. I stood there expecting the ground to swallow me up, though my foot had barely moved since I first wedged it there. I stood there in a field of mud and waved at the houses on the street opposite. Nobody came. Nobody drove by. I suppose there were fewer cars then; we can all say that of our childhoods. I was alone there.

I didn't do well with being left alone. Once in a garden centre I lost sight of my parents. I had been weaving in and out of the little square flowerbeds they had, balancing as though on a tightrope strung across a canyon, and when I looked up my parents had gone. I trampled those perfectly formed flowerbeds, feeling the edges of my vision start to blur; I fell down on the pathway and everything went black. I remember sitting in the boot of the car, my legs dangling, and a woman came up to us and said 'oh dear, is it cancer?' What foolish things adults say.

I stood there, on that muddy patch of land, one boot stuck solid, and for a moment it went completely silent. When I first got married, my wife and I drove up a mountain in Cyprus and got out at the top and it was the most profound silence I had ever experienced. Theresa loved it. She said we should build a cabin there and never go back home, but all I could think of was being stuck in that field in my wellies.

My mum came eventually; it was probably only minutes. Jammy must have called her when he got home. She strode across that field with a smile on her face and asked why I hadn't just lifted my foot out of the welly. I hadn't even thought. I did just that and she pulled my boot out of the ground with a satisfying squelch. That night she got to thinking, why that bit of mud should have sucked me down, and she called the police. That's where they found Susie Banshawe, buried under my boot print.

Her mother came and watched them while they dug; I guess she knew the truth of it somehow. Her cries were so loud they etched on all our brain cells and I hope as I get older they'll be the first ones to go, but I know they won't.

Strangely, it was my father who wanted to move away and Mum who wanted to stay. All her friends were there, she said, and she'd just joined the badminton club. Chasing a ridiculously named piece of plastic twice a week seemed to be more important to her than the safety of her child. I thought briefly that my father's desire to leave was because he had finished Susie Banshawe off himself, but reasoned that if it were true, at least I was in no danger: if he killed his own child it would only draw unwanted attention his way. I don't think there was a man on the estate who people didn't wonder about, which looking back on it is the reason he wanted to leave, I suppose. Their marriage was disintegrating then, perhaps they hadn't really noticed yet, but a few years later and there was no concealing it. I didn't know it then, but when I first saw the cracks starting to show, I wasn't surprised. That's what the whole Susie Banshawe business taught me. I came to see I was always standing on the surface while something unsavoury lurked beneath.

And I tell you her name because I have never forgotten it. Susie Banshawe, Susie Banshawe. When that man did what he did to her he must have thought it would affect her family, that it would affect his own mind, may even have thought of his own family's feelings in the event he was caught. But he won't have thought of a boy running across a muddy field in his new wellies. He won't have considered the effect it would have on me.

They built houses on that field, just as they had planned to. There was talk of a commemorative garden or something, but she'd been dumped off-centre and it spoilt the plans to change the design. Besides, who wanted to buy a new house overlooking a garden in memory of some murdered kid?

We watched the houses go up, but Jammy and I never poked around in those skulls, never jumped out of windows there. We were solemn onlookers. So was Susie Banshawe's mother. She did move away, but she kept coming back, a familiar sight over the years; just standing and watching. Once when Jammy and I stood there a car sped by and one of its hubcaps came off and spun down the road, weaving uncertainly like Mr Pope from number thirty-two on the way back from the pub, finally stopping and doing that thing kids try to do with anything disc shaped and metal: spinning round and round and then clank-clank-clanking against the ground until it stopped. There were long, long seconds of silence then, before Jammy and I hooted with laughter. We howled, we were so happy. It lightened the tone, took away the tension. Jammy took the hubcap home and hung it in his room. His dad humoured him for a week then threw it away or sold it on, who knows.

Now people stand there and say 'before there were houses, this was all fields', all knowing and solemn like there used to be concrete slabs where their houses were built. 'Before there were houses, this was all fields', but you can say that about anywhere, can't you? We all live on old fields, hills, ancient countryside. They even got together to sign a petition to stop the next lot of houses that went up; then the people who moved in there joined in on the petition for the next lot and so it went on. When I'm in bed in my room it's still four walls around me; makes no difference how far the houses stretch down the street. No one stands there and says 'before there were houses, a girl was strangled and buried there,' because it would be unfeeling to the people who have moved in.

I still live on the estate now. I look at those houses, on that ground where my boot print located a dead girl, and I think, 'before I was this, I was something else, something less cluttered.'

We're all something before other things get built on top, things that push down or obscure what was first there. Before we were houses, we were all fields.

I think about myself stuck in that field in my new wellingtons; thinking if I had sunk below the mud I would have sunk right into Susie Banshawe. That thought has kept me awake some nights in my life, I can tell you. And always her mother, standing on the street opposite those houses, in the same way I was with my boots; as if her slightly scuffed black flats have sunk into the tarmac, holding her fast, and she is waiting for rescue.

~

She was not yet ready to let go of her childhood. It was cruel of her father to gather her old toys up when she was out and throw them away.

She shed her tears in private, not wishing him to see how this had hurt her. She wanted to keep just one thing back: a wooden elephant on wheels. This is what she would have chosen. Just one item, a memento. A token to remind her who she had been, how she had felt.

She wondered how this toy could be rescued, remembered how she watched the other children play with the dustbin trucks each Wednesday. She did not like the smell of rotten food. She did not like the men, with their fluorescent clothes, their dirty hands and filthy faces. But she wished to recover her wooden elephant on wheels.

She waited down the side of her house. When the dustman came to pick up the sacks of rubbish at the end of her drive she asked him if he had seen her toy.

'You should come back to my place sometime,' he said. 'The things I find that people throw out, you wouldn't believe.'

He scribbled the address on a scrap of paper and pressed it into her hand.

'What is your name?' he said.

'Susan,' she said. 'But don't tell anyone I spoke to you. I don't want my father to know.'

His house had a sheen of dirt across it as if it worked the dust carts alongside him. Inside you could hardly move. Things were piled up everywhere. She wrinkled her nose at the smell.

'Drink this,' he said, handing her a glass that smelled of the drinks at the back of her father's cabinet. 'I make it myself.'

He showed her some of the things he had rescued from the teeth of his truck. He could see the value of things that were lost, were thrown away; could find some wonder in every item. She felt he too was looking for something he had lost.

All around her the room began to sway. Light reflected from a myriad of metal objects until she felt a million little stars were shining just for her.

Woodwork trains began to trundle along the shelves. Teddy bears clutched at the stuffing bursting from their sides and pushed it back inside, their cheeks burning with shame.

And in the corner of the room, an elephant on wheels raised its trunk and let out a mighty trumpeting sound.

As well as writing short stories, Richard Smyth has written
several history books, and contributes non-fiction to a variety
of publications from the TLS to BBC Wildlife.

Sky Burial

Richard Smyth

They're magnificent birds, they really are. Before you see one in
the flesh you think, well, I'm familiar with buzzards, which are
morphologically similar, so how amazing can it be? It's going to be
a buzzard, basically, only bigger. And then you see one and it's like
nothing you've ever seen before. I mean these birds are *immense*.
I saw my first on the Isle of Rum, years back now, just when the
reintroduction project was getting going. It was being mobbed by a
pair of ravens and it was like a couple of starlings trying to take on
a dragon or something. Huge. Just... just magnificent.

I can see two of them from here — no, three. Two adults and a
juvenile, I think (you can tell the juvenile by its slightly darker tail),

riding the updrafts. Who would ever have thought it, twenty years ago, even ten years ago: white-tailed eagles, over north London?

They are magnificent. But it's different, somehow — they seem less magnificent, when you know that before very long they're going to see you, descend from the sky, and eat you.

Fitting, some people would say. If they were really mean-spirited they'd say: hoist by your own petard, Peter. But that would be unkind. Because of course it was a different world, back then.

I met Grace and then the war happened. There wasn't any connection between the two things; it was just the way it turned out. We had eight months of peace together.

'An aquatic warbler?'

'No. No, just a sedge warbler.' I spoke rather abruptly. The thing was, even though I hardly knew her then, I couldn't bear to see her disappointed. I couldn't bear to have her think that this bird, wriggling in the mist net, was a very rare aquatic warbler, when in fact it was a very common sedge warbler. She was such a beautiful girl.

We were ringing songbirds in the Epping Forest. What you do is, you rig up your mist-net, and you wait for birds to fly into it, and then you grab them, stick a ring on their leg, and let them go again. Grace was very new to the work, hence her elementary error regarding the sedge warbler.

At our wedding, I made a joke of it: something about grabbing her and sticking a ring on her, but in this case having no intention of letting her go again. It got quite a good laugh. But it didn't mean much, because when it came down to it, I did let her go.

We were on honeymoon in the Trossachs when the uprisings began: Kent, Essex, the south-east London sprawl going up in flames. We listened in disbelief to the reports of the first bombings on the radio.

The eagles haven't seen me yet. They're too high. But it's immaterial now, to be honest, because there's something gnawing on my foot. I can't feel my feet but I can feel there's something gnawing on me. I know what it is, too.

I'm not going to look. I don't need to look. I don't want to look. I know what it is.

Even Grace thought we'd gone too far there.

'Look what we achieved with the eagles. Eagles, in Suffolk! Just amazing. And in the Chilterns too, soon. And there are beaver doing very well in Dorset, and there's a very promising breeding programme of Irish elk over in –'

'But *wolves*, Peter. Wolves, in England?'

I can see now that we let our enthusiasm get the better of us. That's the benefit of hindsight. I can see now.

This was a few years after the first wolf reintroductions in Scotland, which were a huge success, of course. 'Rewilding': that was the word on everyone's lips, it was in all the newspapers, people were really excited about it. All the buzzwords: trophic cascades, biodiversity, megafauna. I mean people really wanted it.

Let's reinforce our bond with nature. Let's let the wilderness back in. Let's reconnect with the wildness inside us all.

We had to really battle for it, too. Of course, that's an inappropriate choice of word, in the present circumstances – but we had to struggle, I mean, to get our way. First the New Forest. They were worried about the ponies. They're a tourist attraction, they said. We get thirteen million tourists here a year, they said. And we said, thirteen million people come here every year just to see bloody ponies. Imagine how many you'd get if you had wolves.

And besides, we said – with a confidence that was, I can see now, ill-founded – there'll be fences, wardens, radio collars, real-time tracking.

We had even more of a fight on our hands over the South Downs, with the sheep farmers. They were four-square against the whole idea, but in the end the tourism people took our side, and within a couple of years there it was: wolves, running wild on the Downs. No sheep, of course. But the wolves were magnificent.

I wish I hadn't fallen out with Chris over it, though. I've been thinking a lot about Chris in the last few weeks. Chris was Grace's brother. A soldier — I mean, a real soldier, a professional, a soldier before all this happened.

'It ain't wilderness,' he said.

I bristled.

'Beaver on the Exe. Wolf in the New Forest. Elk, now, in the Forest of Bowland. If that isn't wilderness, Chris, then I don't know what is.'

'You're right.' He drew on his cigarette and smiled. 'You don't know what it is.'

'I think I —'

'Wilderness ain't something you choose, Pete. If you've chose it, it ain't wilderness. Wilderness is the stuff you don't want.'

I was never much enamoured of Chris's seen-it-all tough-guy stylings.

'What we're seeing now,' I said, determinedly keeping my temper under control, 'is England as it was millennia ago. We've rolled back the centuries. All the damage, the exploitation. We've reversed the spread of —' I stopped there, flushing a little, because to my embarrassment the word that had risen to my lips was 'civilisation', and I couldn't think of a better one.

'You're slumming it,' Chris said. He was still smiling. 'You're like when a journalist sleeps rough on the Strand for one night and then says it ain't so bad after all. Because no, it ain't, when you know you've got a warm bed to go back to the next night, a pay-day coming at the end of the month, family to turn to. Fact is,' he said, 'if it ain't so bad, you ain't doing it properly.'

Chris had spent some time sleeping rough at one time, before he joined the Army. I suppose he knew whereof he spoke. I see that now. I wish I had seen it then.

The eagles are lower now. They've probably seen me. Or rather, they've seen — well, they've seen the wolves.

Thank god I can't feel anything. Oh thank god.

I don't want to look. Does that make me a coward? I'm not a coward. I came back, I came back to London, I didn't have to, but I did. I came back, and signed up. I love my country. I'm not embarrassed by that.

Grace didn't like it.

'Your *country*?' We were still in Scotland, still on our honeymoon. I was packing my case. 'Your *country*?' she shouted. 'What the hell, Peter? I mean what the hell does that even mean?'

I thought of eagles and elk and wolves. I thought of the forests and the downs, the rivers and the mountains. I lost my rag a bit, and yelled at her, what do you think this has all been about, Grace, what on earth do you think I've been working for, all these years?

She pursed her lips and didn't answer. And when I came back, she came back with me. She was my wife, after all.

I am being dragged across the car park, slowly, doggedly, by my left foot. There's no pain. I close my eyes.

The first time they bombed Archway, Grace was upstairs and I was downstairs. A big hit, a direct hit.

I suppose you want me to explain it. The revolution, the war. The reason why this was happening: English killing English, here in England, English bullets, English blood.

And of course, I would explain it, if I could. But you know already why I can't. It came from somewhere else — or rather, it came from here, right here, but somehow, in some way I can't explain, it wasn't mine. Or perhaps it was but I didn't feel as though it was.

'England, your England,' she'd said, somewhat spitefully, when we'd crossed the border on our way home from our honeymoon. I don't know what she meant by that because she was as English as I was. I asked her as I drove, tense myself from the news and the blinding rain and the military checkpoints along the A74, *what, what do you mean?* But she wouldn't say, just sat there thin-lipped in the passenger seat with her arms folded, watching the wipers.

'It's not mine,' I said. 'It's ours. Not just yours and mine, although it's that too, but all of ours. Everyone's. England, *our* England,' I said.

She was upstairs when the bomb hit.

It was a physical sensation, a terrible deep riptide through the air and through my body, before it was anything else. Then it was a noise like the world's ending.

When I came to I found that there was no upstairs left. No Grace either. I stood at the top of our stairs beneath the blue sky and wished that I had been upstairs and she had been downstairs. I watched red kites circle in the smoke rising over the shopping centre. It was the day before I was due to start basic training.

We didn't see it coming. That's all there is to it. I can admit that now. For all our impact assessments, all our site inspections, all our contingency plans; we didn't see it coming. I don't mean the bombing, I don't even mean the civil war — I mean the wilderness, the real wilderness, the wilderness Chris knew about.

My head's knocking on pitted asphalt. I open my eyes. I still won't look — I don't want to meet its gaze (have you ever had that nightmare?) — but I want to see the sky.

The car park is vast, grey, long deserted, the white lines faded, purple cones of buddleia nodding in clumps, dandelions sprouting through the asphalt.

This is the wilderness. It always was. Wilderness is what you don't see, what you don't want to see — it's what you can't do a damn thing about. These acres of dereliction, given over to the buddleia, the starlings, the lichen, the London drizzle. Car parks, empty factories, abandoned footings, grey scrapes of earth where buildings have been demolished and not rebuilt, sallow sidings of rubble and weed, broken floors of concrete fenced with barbed wire and straggly elder. And it gets bigger and bigger and worse and worse, it crowds in on us, all of us, and we simply can't stop it.

I thought I was fighting for England when I led the raid on the bunker they'd dug in on the Holloway Road. And when the shrapnel took me in the back I thought it was England I was dying for.

Grace was right. I didn't know what England even meant.

I've stopped. I mean, we've stopped. It's stopped, in the shade of a forest of musty-smelling rosebay willowherb. I can still see the sky. I can see the eagles. They're so close now I can see each feather. They're still magnificent. I've been wrong about a lot of things, I can see that now, but they're still magnificent.

I lift my head. It's an effort. I lift my head and I look at the wolf. The wolf looks back at me.

Louis Rakovich's haunting and atmospheric story is his first appearance in our anthology series.

Jonathan

Louis Rakovich

It was a four-hour drive to the lake. Danielle suggested he go by plane, and he frowned the way he always did when he wanted her to stop pestering him. She smiled and said very quietly, 'By car it is.' He thought she battled him through every step of the preparations – booking the cabin, packing, setting the alarm clock on his last night at home – only to surrender each time. She must have thought he was stubborn, and maybe it was true, but he had a right to be. It was his sixtieth birthday.

Maurice remembered the scenic route from many years ago. It hadn't changed. Still the same firs, two hundred feet high – he could never lift his head high enough to see their tops from the road — and the purple coned spruces. He had been to many lakes through the years. He didn't know why he picked this one now. Perhaps because he hadn't been there the longest, perhaps because it was the first to come to his mind with the idea of the fishing trip.

Each time he stopped to stretch his legs he thanked the gods for the sunny weather. When he arrived at last, the sun was high in the sky, and the firs stood below it like an unconquerable green cliff. He entered the reception office, which seemed to double as a convenience store, and introduced himself. The man behind the counter, perhaps eighty years old, had a blissfully lazy look on his face. He got up heavily and handed Maurice his key.

'Yours is the white one there, see it?' He pointed through the window to a lone cabin by the pier.

Maurice drove up to the cabin and brought his picnic cooler and fishing equipment inside. He passed through the living room, paying little attention to his surroundings, and went out to the porch. His view for the next three days opened before him. He set down the cooler, the fishing rod, and the bait box, and fell into a soft wicker recliner. The boat tied to the pier swayed just barely in the calm water. Three other cabins stood scattered in the distance. He was as alone as he could be in a place like this, and it was good.

He took the boat to a spot near the centre of the lake, where he thought he'd seen some splashing, and cast his bait. In the first twenty minutes he caught and released a big largemouth bass whose face reminded him of his wife's first husband, then nothing for three hours. The ride had tired him more than he cared to admit, and he found himself drifting off to sleep.

He woke up some time later; it couldn't have been very late, for the sky was bright blue and the sun shone somewhere behind the tops of the firs. There was a movement in his hand, something pulling at the line. He reeled it in and pulled out an enormous dark bowfin. It struggled in his grip and flapped its backside even as he tried to release the hook from the roof of its mouth. Strange, he thought, did bowfins even swim in deep waters? He released the hook and studied the fish.

'Nice,' said a voice to his left.

The fish dropped out of his hands and hit the edge of the boat with a loud wet thud before tumbling into the water. Maurice's skin grew cold. He knew that voice.

He turned his head slowly. Jonathan was sitting by his side, smiling as though in approval of his catch. He looked down and gestured with his head toward the bait box. The fish had knocked it open when it hit the boat.

'It's all right,' Maurice said, hearing himself through a fog. 'It's okay, I'll clean it up.'

He bent down and scooped the worms back into the box. He shook his hand over the edge and two small worms dropped into the water. A mouth came up to just below the surface and swallowed them, then disappeared back into the depths.

Jonathan looked up, squinting at the sun. He seemed healthy, the way he was before everything. He must have been about thirty years old.

Maurice swallowed the lump in his throat, then coughed. 'Am I dead?'

Jonathan chuckled. 'It's a beautiful place, isn't it?'

'What?'

'The place, completely unspoiled.'

'Yes.'

They sat in silence for a little while. Then Jonathan smiled and nodded toward the fishing rod.

'What are you waiting for?' he asked. 'You won't have anything to eat.'

'No, it's... I do catch and release.'

'Yeah? Throw them right back in?'

'Yes.'

'Still, that's what we're here for.'

Maurice held the rod and tried handing it over, but Jonathan lifted his hand to stop him and shook his head.

'I'm all right. I'll just watch you.'

He cast the bait. For a long while there was nothing, and he was becoming very nervous. When at last something pulled at the line he felt an unexplained relief. What did he care whether he caught a fish or not? Yet his mouth was dry and his hands trembled wildly as he reeled it in: an ugly little trout. He lifted it to show to Jonathan, then threw it back in the water. 'Let's go to shore,' he said.

He went to the bathroom, leaving Jonathan alone in the living room. He turned on the water in the sink and sat down on the edge of the tub. Nothing was keeping him here; he could take his things and walk right out the door to his car, and it would be as if none of this had happened. But a part of him wanted to stay and soak in the fear and the guilt that the man in the living room brought up in him. It was the same compulsion that had made him as a child unable to wait for a scab to heal before tearing it off, the same strange desire for the unpleasant that made him engage in the same fight over and over again with Danielle.

He went back into the living room. Jonathan was standing with his face to the window, his hands held together behind his back.

'So I guess you'll be staying the night here,' Maurice said.

There was no answer.

'There's only one bed, but... we've made do with worse in the past. There's the couch.'

Still there was no answer, and the man stood unmoving, refusing to turn around. Maurice grew scared.

'Please look at me.'

He did. In the second after Jonathan began to turn and before his face became visible, Maurice imagined all the terrible forms he might take. His face could be a bare skull, or worse still, the thin, grey, living face Maurice hadn't stayed long enough to see. But he was just his old self, the same as earlier on the boat.

Maurice approached him and put his hands on his shoulders, then grabbed him by the hair, gently, and looked into his eyes.

'Jonathan, I'm so sorry.'

He let go of Jonathan's hair, put one hand on the back of his head and pulled him closer. He kissed him, and Jonathan opened his mouth very slowly, and looked into his eyes all the while. Maurice let go. There was something disgusting about this fish-eyed passivity.

Maurice took a step back and cleared his throat. 'Dinner. Do you want to eat? There's a restaurant, by the water there.' He pointed at the wall behind him without looking. 'But we would have to go there. Or, or I can go without you and take it to go. There's a... Oh, there's a fridge. A mini fridge.' He looked at the white box, suddenly very tired again. 'Do you want to eat?'

'No, I'm not hungry. You go ahead.'

Maurice's knees trembled. He was scared to the marrow of his bones – of Jonathan, and of the stupid and mundane words coming out of his own mouth. He closed his eyes and breathed in, trying to pull himself together.

'What are you doing here, after all this time? Why couldn't you leave me in peace?'

Jonathan sat on the couch. 'I died here.'

'Where, here?'

'On that lake.'

'How is that possible?' Maurice sat down on the arm of the couch, far from Jonathan.

'I remembered you telling me about this place,' Jonathan said. 'How big the rainbow trout are, and so many fish, how they all but jump into your boat. And I thought, what the hell, I might as well catch some before I die.'

'Did you?'

'Yes, quite the bunch. Funny thing,' he smiled, and Maurice's skin flushed with shame, 'I threw them all back. Not because I was doing what you do. I just knew it would be a waste of fish, even if I did live long enough to eat them. But I didn't. Died right in the boat.'

There was a silence. Maurice felt a pressure in his nose which he hadn't felt in years. The cloth of his undershirt clung to his skin and all his organs were hot inside, but his hands were ice cold.

'You're wearing that shirt,' he said.

Jonathan looked down. 'What shirt?'

'The one I burned.'

'Oh. Well, it was my favourite shirt. Why did you burn it?'

'You left it in my house. I only found it much later, under the bed.'

'Oh.'

He was too tired to think anymore. Only one thought remained in his mind, and he spoke it out loud, slowly, in an unchanging tone. 'I'm going to hell.'

Someone knocked on the door. Maurice jumped up so fast his vision went black.

'Who's there?'

'Room service.'

Puzzled, he opened the door. The old man from the reception desk stood on the doorstep, holding a small glass jar filled with something lumpy and brown.

'I forgot to give you your welcome gift,' he said. 'We give it to all our guests. Here.'

Maurice looked down at the tag and forced a smile. 'One Hundred First Class Worms?'

'Best in the country.'

'Really?'

'Really. No one grows them better than my wife. Holds them in a big tank, just the right temperature. Feeds them all kinds of healthy stuff, peppers and avocados and whatnot. Look how fat.'

Maurice brought the jar closer to his eyes.

'Yes,' he said. 'Thank you very much. Will come in handy tomorrow.'

The man's eyes pointed behind Maurice's shoulder. 'Is the room all right?'

'Yes, I...' Maurice looked back. The room was empty. 'Yes, everything's fine.'

'Good,' said the man. 'Well, I'll be off.'

He turned around and went down the steps. Maurice put the worm jar on top of the fridge, then froze a moment and ran out of the cabin. The man was getting into his car.

'Wait.'

'Anything wrong?'

'No, not at all. But, can I ask you something?'

The man seemed amused. 'Sure thing.'

'How long have you worked here?'

'Wow, quite a long time, sir. When I started here it was, what, forty years ago, a little more. But that was before my wife and I bought the place. I was just an employee first, you know, hired help. Cleaned the cabins, manned the register when the cashier was sick. But you know how those things are, someone doesn't come one day, you get some of their work thrown at you, bit by bit, and you find yourself managing the place, you know? Then the old owner wants to sell and retire, and you think – I think – I like the work, might as well stay here with the wife, hire some young folk to do the heavy lifting.' He smiled. 'Why do you ask?'

'Is it true thirty years ago someone died on the lake?'

'Who told you?'

'Just someone.'

'Well, yes, it's true, but I don't want you to think he drowned or anything like that. Nothing like that at all. He was a sick man, very sick.'

'He died right in his boat?'

The man sighed. 'Yeah. Poor girl, the one who found him. I knew her, a waitress at the restaurant. She was the kind who scream whenever they see a spider – you know those people. But she didn't scream when she saw him, and that says something. Because the sight was truly an unpleasant one. Black circles under the eyes, and so thin you could almost see the lines of his teeth through his cheeks. We called the police...'

Maurice stopped listening.

He returned to the empty cabin. He looked in the bedroom, in the bathroom and on the porch, but Jonathan wasn't there. He lay on the bed without taking his clothes off, and fell asleep a few minutes later. He dreamed that a spider made of human teeth crawled into his mouth.

He woke up a few minutes before seven. One half of the lake stood in the shadow of the firs, the other half in the sun.

Somewhere on the sunny shore a family was laying out towels and sticking a beach umbrella into the ground.

He took the First Class Worms on the boat with him, and headed to where the shadow met the light. The worms were fat and soft, and apparently the fish liked them, for he caught a large bass in the first twenty minutes, just like the previous day, then two rainbow trout, and another bass. But no bowfins.

Two hours went by. He began to doubt that Jonathan would show up again, but there was no relief in that thought. Something pulled at the line and he didn't rush to reel it in. He wondered whether he would stay the third day. Then someone said, 'Well, go on. Let's see who that is.'

Maurice turned to look at Jonathan. He was half smiling, looking at the water intently. His eyelashes cast thin shadows on the whites of his eyes, and his blue irises were bright under the sun, as though illuminated from within. Many years ago Maurice couldn't see him like that without loving him, without imagining those eyes staring at some bedroom ceiling, gleaming, bloodshot; the lips parted, the teeth white and wet; gasping, his chest rising and falling under Maurice's chest.

'Go on,' Jonathan repeated.

Maurice blinked. There was only guilt now. He pulled the fish out and held it up under the light. Another trout.

Jonathan whistled. 'Beautiful fella.'

Maurice threw it back in the water. 'Look,' he said, 'I want you to understand. I loved you, I just —'

'Forget about it.'

'No, I shouldn't have left you to die alone. I know I deserve to burn for it, but if you could forgive me somehow.'

'Maurice.'

The sound of his name was terrifying coming from this man's mouth.

'What?'

'Are you going to catch another damn fish or not?'

Maurice took a worm out of the jar, pierced it, did a half hitch knot and cast it into the water. He reached for the cooler behind him and took out two beer cans. He opened one, then the other, and pushed the latter toward Jonathan.

'You don't have to drink yours,' he said. 'Just let it sit there.'

The sky was bright and the sun shone high for most of the afternoon. They caught four basses, four trout, and one yellow perch the size of a man's hand.

About the Contributors

Adam Blampied has been writing live comedy as part of The Beta Males since 2008 and fiction on his lonesome since 2012. He won the Four Stories screenwriting competition in 2012, the 2013 Mardibooks short story competition and was recently shortlisted for The Fiction Desk Newcomer Prize 2015, for 'The Cobble Boys'.

He has written his first play, called *A Good Hiding*, and will also be taking his first standup hour to the Edinburgh Fringe this year, called *I Am Mr Children Man*.

Die Booth lives in Chester and enjoys tea, cake, and exploring dark places. Die's short stories have featured in publications by Black & BLUE, *Litro*, Prime, and The Cheshire Prize for

Literature. You can read more of Die's writing in debut novel *Spirit Houses*, and in *365 Lies*: a single author collection of one flash fiction for every day of the year, out now in support of the MNDA. 'Whole Wide World' is Die's fourth Fiction Desk story.

Jacki Donnellan's stories have been published in several magazines and anthologies, both online and in print, and she has won several flash fiction contests. She is one of the original members of the Flashdogs online flash fiction community with stories in both the first and second volumes of the Flashdogs anthologies. Jacki is British and lives in the Netherlands with her husband and two teenage children. She can be found on Twitter at @Donnellanjacki.

Tim Dunbar lives in Denver, Colorado. He writes short fiction, poetry, and is working on his first novel. 'A Series of Circles' is his first published story. Married with two kids, Tim works full-time as a finance director at a local nonprofit and is pursuing ordination as a deacon in the Episcopal Church. He can be found on the web at www.timothydunbar.com and on Twitter at @TimDunbarDenver.

Matthew Licht is the author of *West Ways* (Christoph Keller Editions / JRP Ringier; the imaginary adventures of Mae West and a young fighter pilot), and several other novels. His two short story collections with Salt, *The Moose Show* and *Justine, Joe & The Zen Garbageman*, have been nominated for the Frank O'Connor Prize. His two-wheel obsession is unspooling into a literary monster known as *CyclOps*.

Matthew's story 'Dave Tough's Luck' appeared in *Various Authors*, the first Fiction Desk anthology. 'Across the Kinderhook' appeared in *Crying Just Like Anybody*, and 'Washout' appeared in *New Ghost Stories*. *New Ghost Stories II* featured his story 'The Bear Got Me'.

S R Mastrantone writes, and spends too much time thinking about dinosaurs, in Oxford. His stories have been published or are forthcoming in *Press Start to Play* (Vintage / Random House), *Lamplight*, *carte blanche*, and *Shock Totem*. He is a past winner of The Fiction Desk Writer's Award, and placed second in our 2015 Ghost Story competition. He is working on his first novel.

Mark Newman has been shortlisted for the Costa Short Story Award, highly commended in the New Writer Prose & Poetry Awards, and Bristol Prize longlisted. His work has won competitions judged by Alison Moore, Tania Hershman, and David Gaffney. He has been published in *Firewords Quarterly*, *Paper Swans*, and has eight stories in the Retreat West competition anthology *Inside These Tangles, Beauty Lies*. His Twitter account is @mn73.

Louis Rakovich writes sometimes-fantastical literary fiction. His short stories have appeared in numerous publications, including *Bartleby Snopes*, *Criminal Element*, *Goldfish Grimm*, *Phobos Magazine* and *Spark: A Creative Anthology*. He's inspired by authors such as Truman Capote, Gabriel Garcia Marquez and Edgar Poe, and filmmakers such as David Lynch and Andrei Tarkovsky. He grew up in Jerusalem, Israel, and currently lives in NYC, where he's working on his first novel – a psychological thriller with theological undertones. You can find more stories by him at www.louisrakovich.com, or follow him on Twitter at @LouisRakovich.

Richard Smyth's first novel, *Wild Ink*, was published in 2014 by Dead Ink Books. His prize-winning short fiction has appeared in *The Stinging Fly*, *The Stockholm Review*, *Litro*, *Riptide*, *Firewords*, and two anthologies from Arachne Press; as a journalist and critic, he has written for the *TLS*, *New Scientist*, *New Humanist*, *BBC Wildlife* and many more. He lives in West Yorkshire.

His previous stories for The Fiction Desk are 'Chalklands' (*New Ghost Stories*) and the title story from *Crying Just Like Anybody*.

For more information on the contributors
to this volume, please visit our website:

www.thefictiondesk.com/authors

Also Available

the first eight Fiction Desk anthologies:

Subscribe

three volumes
for just £22

(in the UK, or £29 worldwide).

Subscribing to our anthology series is the best way to keep yourself supplied with the best new short fiction from the UK and abroad. It costs just £22 for three volumes within the UK, or £29 for a worldwide subscription.

(Prices correct at time of going to press, but may change
over time; please see website for current pricing.)

www.thefictiondesk.com